**"I know what you came for," he said.**

"I didn't come for that either," I said. "You don't know me, Hades. Even if you think that you do."

"I've been your lover for a decade, *agape*. Don't tell me that I don't know you. I know every sigh, every scream. I know the way that your blue eyes darken when you need me. I know just how dark your fantasies are. How the cold, calculated businesswoman likes for someone to tell her what to do as long as she's naked. How you wish for someone to tie you down and make your decisions for you. I don't just know what you want, Florence. I know what you beg for."

He made my knees weak. But while I had been weak with him for all of these years, I wouldn't be weak now. There was too much at stake.

"I came because I have to tell you something. I'm pregnant, Hades. I'm having your baby."

He stood there. Immobilized. He said nothing. For one long minute, he said nothing. And then, he looked at me. With a black fire that chilled me to my soul.

"This changes everything."

**Maisey Yates** is the *New York Times* bestselling author of over one hundred romance novels. An avid knitter with a dangerous yarn addiction and an aversion to housework, Maisey lives with her husband and three kids in rural Oregon. She believes the trek she makes to her coffee maker each morning is a true example of her pioneer spirit. Find out more about Maisey's books on her website, maiseyyates.com, or find her on Facebook, Instagram or TikTok by searching her name.

**Books by Maisey Yates**

**Harlequin Presents**

*Crowned for My Royal Baby*
*The Secret That Shocked Cinderella*

***The Heirs of Liri***

*His Majesty's Forbidden Temptation*
*A Bride for the Lost King*

***Pregnant Princesses***

*Crowned for His Christmas Baby*

***The Royal Desert Legacy***

*Forbidden to the Desert Prince*
*A Virgin for the Desert King*

***A Diamond in the Rough***

*The Italian's Pregnant Enemy*

Visit the Author Profile page
at Harlequin.com for more titles.

# PREGNANT ENEMY, CHRISTMAS BRIDE

MAISEY YATES

PRESENTS

ISBN-13: 978-1-335-93931-9

Pregnant Enemy, Christmas Bride



For questions and comments about the quality of this book, please contact us at CustomerService@Harlequin.com.

Harlequin Enterprises ULC
22 Adelaide St. West, 41st Floor
Toronto, Ontario M5H 4E3, Canada
www.Harlequin.com

**Printed in Lithuania**

# PREGNANT ENEMY, CHRISTMAS BRIDE

To mad sparks of creativity that take us unexpected places. This book was the greatest gift to me right when I needed it.

# CHAPTER ONE

I CLUTCHED THE strap of my shoulder bag as I waited for the elevator to reach its floor. I was far more nervous than I should be, given that I was prepared—if not overly prepared—for this.

The adrenaline in my veins was more energizing than any hit of caffeine, more electrifying than any shot of whiskey. It flooded me now, making it impossible for me to stand still. Thankfully the elevator was empty, so I had no audience as I bounced on the balls of my feet as I waited. And waited.

I would never dare show even a hint of nerves, excitement or any other emotion in a public space, where the media might take it and spin it out of control.

*Florence Clare is a Head Case! We Knew it All Along!*

*Clare Heir Succumbs to Feelings!*

*Are Women Too Emotional To Be CEOs?*

I would rather die.

Okay, not *die*. But I'd hate it.

The floor number illuminated on the panel. A sound chimed. I checked my reflection.

Not a hair out of place. I could never risk being

anything like a human woman. I had to be CEO Barbie. Just pretty enough, just soft enough, just tough enough. It wasn't fair, but nothing in life was. I was privileged and I knew it. So I wasn't going to waste time whining about the inequality I experienced when there were other women in much more dire straits than I. All I could do was try to change it by succeeding.

This was for a NASA contract. The press would be there.

And they were expecting a show.

I was ready to give them one.

I stepped out of the elevator and swept down the hall. I knew I looked flawless in my black suit, perfectly tailored, perfectly pressed. Not a wrinkle to be seen.

I'd better. I spent the whole drive from the hotel lying down flat in the back seat to keep everything from creasing. I'd practically rolled out of the car in the private garage my driver had pulled into.

For the last five years every move I'd made had been so high profile I couldn't even risk a sneeze at the wrong moment. Even that could be spun into a story about me. A badly timed photo could result in a headline about me crying or yelling at someone.

A photo taken at midsneeze painted a thousand lying words.

I knew this for certain.

Ever since my father had died and I'd taken over Edison Inc, I'd been under a microscope. But I'd trained for it my whole life.

And the truth was, I loved it.

All right, not every part of it. But enough of it.

I liked to imagine this was what it must be like to be a bullfighter. To be a boxer. An MMA fighter, even. To get high on adrenaline, anticipating the battle. To be enthralled by the roar of the crowd.

To crave the fight. The impact of your fist hitting your opponent.

Oh, yes, I craved that most of all.

I moved closer to the doors of the conference room.

My heart surged. I smiled. Flawless, like I had to be.

Invulnerable.

That was the image I had to portray. As a woman, possessing beauty was useful. But beauty was a mask that could be put on in the morning and taken off with makeup remover. Beauty was in the way clothing was tailored.

The real trick, the real necessity, was to never, ever show them a weakness.

As a woman who ran one of the single largest conglomerates in the world, I had to be feminine, beautiful, and give the idea that I might be soft. I also had to essentially be a man in lipstick. I could never have real, female attributes. I couldn't have a pimple lest someone guess I was nearing my period, nor could I ever have an emotional outburst for the same reason. I had to be a woman in name and appearance only or my competence would be called into question.

I never allowed that to happen.

Two men flanking the doors moved to open them as I drew near, and time stood still.

This was the pause before the battle began to rage.

I would meet my enemy in that room for the first of a series of presentations where we tried to get the lucrative NASA contracts based on the rocket technology our individual companies had cultivated.

The media seemed to think I might be upset to have to go up against him again.

In truth, I relished it.

I never wanted to fight below my weight class.

I might hate *him* with very nearly the whole of my being. But he was also the only man who was strong enough to make it war.

In business, war was the only way it was fun.

My foot crossed the threshold of the room and time returned to normal. Cameras were raised, my photo was taken. I turned my head, and there he was.

Hades Achelleos.

The devil himself.

He was dressed all in black, just as I was, his dark hair swept back from his forehead. He had a fallen angel face, so beautiful he was almost unnerving to look at—or so many in the media had written in prose bordering on purple, I thought.

It was true, his cheekbones were sharp, his jaw square. He was tall and muscular. All of the things considered conventionally attractive in a man.

I had first met him when he was seventeen and I was fourteen. A massive charity event we'd been dragged to by our fathers. Our fathers, Theseus Achelleos and Martin Clare, had hated each other. As much as they had loved to fight one another.

The rivalry between their companies was the stuff of corporate legend.

Both starting out with hotel chains, expanding to travel—cruise ships, airlines, energy. What one did, the other would follow and try to improve on. Until they'd arrived where they were now. Unquestionably at the top of the industry with their children at the helm. Carrying on both their legacies and the vicious, cutthroat rivalry they had so cherished.

I'd been prejudiced against him before the first meeting. He had, all the years since, made certain that I hated him not simply because of his legacy, but because of *everything* about him.

Arrogant.

Insufferable.

The actual god of hell.

"Hello, Miss Clare." He stepped forward and reached out his hand.

I shook it. As I'd done a thousand times before. "Mr. Achelleos."

The room was filled with scientists, engineers, media and investors. It was set up for a panel-style talk, which would make it something like a debate.

Excitement ignited in my blood. Hades and I both made our way to the front of the room and took our seats. I looked at him. My stomach churned. Even his profile was arrogant.

He looked at me out of the corner of his eye, and the glint there, the certainty, it made me want to fight him even harder.

We were introduced to the crowd by a moderator—

the introduction a formality. Everyone knew who we were.

And then it was time.

"Edison Inc is in the perfect position to pioneer the next wave of space exploration. Our commercial space travel has been successful, with our next prototype indicating that it will be possible to increase the accessibility of space flights."

"All well and good," Hades said, cutting me off. "But does space need to be accessible to the masses, or does it need to remain the bastion of scientists? It isn't as though British tourists can go lay on the sands of Mars."

He infuriated me.

"That is not the intent of space travel, and I think you know that. Surely, Mr. Achelleos, you are not so out of touch that you believe education is the province of the überwealthy?"

"I don't believe that's what I said, Miss Clare, rather I am simply suggesting that, like the Great Barrier Reef and the Arctic, there is merit in keeping masses of humans from crawling all over something unspoiled like ants at a picnic."

I hated him for that. As much as his acidic words ignited a fire in me. A fire I loved. A fire I needed.

I sometimes wondered if it would be possible to function as well as I did if it weren't for the sheer hatred of him. The electric excitement of having a nemesis.

"Are you bringing something to the table, Mr.

Achelleos, or are you simply here to insult what I've brought?"

He shifted, directing his focus to the audience. "I am not putting resources into the commercialization of space. Rather what Mercury is focusing on is creating spacecraft with the very highest standard of scientific instruments on board."

As if I hadn't thought that NASA was going to need scientific instruments. Which I said, though not like an indignant teenager. Even if that was how I felt. How he made me feel. Like all my emotions were just beneath the surface of my skin. Reckless, unwieldy, like they never otherwise were.

We went back and forth, each shot like a blow in the ring. The slice of a knife.

"Arrogance. The assumption that access is equal to loss is the very height of privilege."

"Idealism that science can't afford."

*Left hook. Right hook.*

"Idealism is part of space exploration, Hades."

*Uppercut.*

"And practicality is what prevents catastrophe, Florence."

Finally our hour had concluded. The room exploded with applause and flashes, and my vision blurred for a moment as my heart beat a wild cadence that left me feeling dizzy.

Everything slowed. I looked at him. He looked back.

Those black eyes were always fathomless.

I could hear my own heartbeat. For a moment I thought I could hear his.

Then everything sped up again.

"Miss Clare!" came the shout of a reporter. "If you don't win the contract with NASA, will that halt the space arm of Edison?"

I turned my full focus to the reporter. "Absolutely not. We're committed to staying on the cutting edge of what's happening in the world of travel. The ground-breaking science we've employed in our rocket program has led to things like longer commercial airline flights, faster airplanes. It is research that has resonance in other parts of the industry."

"Mr. Achelleos! If you get the contract what will that mean for the Super Ship set to be unveiled in four years' time?"

Hades slashed his hand to the side as if he was cutting through vines in the jungle. "The funding for the Super Ship is entirely separate. We are equipped and have the resources to make multiple breakthroughs at once."

"I see that the ocean is not as sacred to you as space, Mr. Achelleos?" I asked.

"I don't see a press badge, Miss Clare." His eyes dipped to my breasts, as if he were searching for credentials. I ignored the way his dark gaze made my skin burn and my breasts feel heavy.

"I would like to ask you a question," I said, turning from Hades and to the reporter who had just spoken to us both. "Why is it you asked me what I'd do if I lost, and what he would do if he won? Does his gender make this a foregone conclusion for you?"

The reporter sputtered. "No, not at all, only..."

"Perhaps it was the quality of my performance," Hades said.

"Or perhaps what you have in your trousers," I said, icy.

He stared at me for a breath. Then another.

*You know what I meant.* I thought that, as if he could hear me.

I wasn't thinking about his... I was only saying it was a sexist line of questioning and Hades should well know it.

Questions came fast and frequent after that and we could barely get a breath. By the time it was done I was stratospheric. It was unlike anything else. Riding into battle to face Hades.

Iron sharpened iron. And we were both as inflexible as the hardest steel.

We rose from the table and shook hands again. I walked ahead of him down the aisle and got into the elevator. The doors closed behind me.

The silence was like a blanket, settling over me. Smothering me.

My ears buzzed. It was so jarring to be in the quiet, the stillness, after such a frenetic hour.

We wouldn't know about the contract until we had another few presentations. The next one wouldn't be public. I already had everything prepared.

The elevator reached the bottom floor and the doors

opened. I walked out of the building and straight to the black car that was waiting for me.

I opened up my phone and checked the details. "The Tomlin."

*Penthouse One.*

The virtual key was already on my phone so I would be able to go straight up without stopping at the front desk. Good.

Traffic was hellish, but that was DC.

I opened up my compact and refreshed my red lipstick. I eyed my overnight bag, considering changing en route, rather than getting out of the car in what would now be a rumpled suit. But now with the meeting behind me, some of my edges had been dulled. I didn't want to wrestle with getting the suit off, especially not with the elaborate undergarments I had underneath. No thanks.

While the car crawled through traffic, I replayed the whole thing in my mind.

The way he'd looked when I'd gotten a shot in. The relish when he'd lobbed one back.

I felt my adrenaline start to peak again as the car pulled up to the historic building in Georgetown. Red brick with stark white windows.

I took my purse and my overnight bag and got out of the car, assuring the bellhops that I did not need assistance as I went inside then into another elevator. It only took a moment to get to the top level of the building—there were only twelve of them—and I stepped out and onto the glossy marble floor, making my way to the room all the way at the end of the hall and unlocking it via my phone.

It was gorgeous. The chaise lounge by the window was plush and perfect. I moved into the bedroom and saw a giant four-poster bed. I walked inside and dragged my fingertips along the velvet. Then I touched the glossy wood on the bed frame.

I heard a sound in the next room and paused.

I turned and walked back into the living room, just as the door was closing.

And there he was. Dressed all in black.

My heart leaped into my throat.

"Hades."

It was time for the real battle to begin.

# CHAPTER TWO

"TRAFFIC WAS A NIGHTMARE," he said, beginning to loosen his tie.

"I know."

And my adrenaline hit its peak.

Because this was what we'd been walking toward all day. This was the real show. The one no one else would see. The one no one else would ever know about.

Through the haze that was beginning to descend I did think to ask about practicalities. "The room is registered under…?"

"Neither of our names."

"And you…?"

"Came in the back."

Hades Achelleos was a man of aristocratic and noble blood. But he walked through staff-only entrances, fire exits and side doors in alleyways for this.

For me.

It would be tempting to take that personally. But I knew from experience that with Hades nothing was personal. Especially when it felt like it might burn me alive.

He was fire personified. He couldn't help it if he scalded everything he touched.

Sometimes I told myself, if I could go back to the moment when I'd first ruined everything, ruined us, I would. That I would make a different choice that night.

Lose my virginity to a waiter or some random dude I met on the beach.

But in my heart I knew I wouldn't.

Because doing battle with him in a boardroom was a high. But this was everything.

He crossed the room, his movements silken, like a big cat stalking his prey. Prey would run, though. And I wasn't running.

When he closed the distance between us, the move was lightning fast, his lips crashing down on mine the moment he brought me up against his hard body.

*Victory.*

I had him under my spell as much as he had me under his, and so while I sometimes felt helpless, a junkie addicted to his brand of pleasure, I knew he was no better. And that sustained me.

We were the only two people on earth equally matched to each other. In business and in the bedroom.

He propelled me back against the wall, his hands rough on my curves as he tore at my clothes. My perfectly tailored suit that I'd been so careful not to crease. He wrenched it from my body and left it on the floor like it was nothing.

And revealed what I had on underneath. What I'd

had on the whole time. The look on his face was feral. I hadn't changed into a dress in the back of the car because it had felt too fussy, but what I hadn't counted on was this moment. I was glad then that I hadn't changed. Because this way he knew.

"You were wearing this the whole time?"

A corseted top with lace cups that were completely see-through and a lace thong to match. Garters and stockings. The sort of thing he'd said he found too elaborate to be practical when all he wanted was to be inside me.

I knew Hades well enough to know that if I did not oppose him, it wouldn't be as thrilling. Sometimes I gave him what he wanted. Me. Bare beneath my clothes so that there was no waiting. And sometimes….

If it wasn't rough, it wasn't fun.

So sometimes I liked to goad him.

Push him. Find his limits.

I nodded slowly.

He gripped my chin and forced my face to tilt upward, to meet his gaze. "You are wicked, do you know that?"

"That's what you like."

He was kissing me again, and it was such a rush. Such a relief. To be trapped between the unforgiving wall and the hardness of his chest. To be in his arms.

It had been a month since we'd last done this. And every day since had been like torture. I'd thought of what we would do, and how it would be. What the room would look like. When I'd walked in and spotted the chaise, I'd known what he intended to do with that. He would put me on my hands and knees and use the shape of the lounge to make it easier for him to take me from behind.

Then the four-poster bed…oh, yes, I'd known his intent for that too.

I would likely spend the night tied to it.

But first…first this. This runaway freight train of desire. It had to be dealt with. It had to be satisfied. Hot. Quick. Fast.

I felt his own desperation matching my own.

He moved his hands down my body then up again to cup my breasts, his large palms rough as he held me, squeezed me, while he left a blazing hot trail of kisses down my neck.

I moved my own hands then, ripping at his tie, at his crisp white shirt. Shedding his layers as I shed mine. As he left me in nothing but the thong and stockings. His body was so hard, so muscular.

Over the years it had changed.

I could remember him at twenty-one. Ten years ago. Lean and lithe, and the most beautiful thing I'd ever seen. Obsessed with him. It had been embarrassing.

Back then I'd had the dirtiest sexual fantasies of any virgin alive because my fantasies had starred Hades. And even a virgin couldn't make him innocuous.

He was broader now. Bigger. Harder. His chest had dark hair on it that extended down to his perfect, ridged abdomen.

My eyes met his and the breath left my lungs. How

did he still take my breath away? Maybe more now than he had then. Maybe more now than ever before.

He pushed his hands between my legs, where I knew he would find me wet and needy. How could I be anything else? There was no need for foreplay. We'd just had hours of it.

Watching him answer every question with ease. Using his sharp intellect to cut everyone around him, including me. I gave as good as I got, I always did. With everyone and everything, but most of all with Hades. Most of all with him.

I brought my hand down to cup his arousal and he growled, leaning in and biting my neck as he stroked me between my thighs. The pleasure was white-hot, so intense. More, better than it had ever been. Or maybe I just couldn't remember anything but right now.

One blunt finger found the entrance to my body, and as he moved it inside of me, he kept his eyes on mine.

"This is what you wanted the whole time, isn't it?" he asked, his voice rough. "When you were sitting there answering their questions all you really thought of was having me inside you."

"It's true," I said, my voice a thready whisper. "But you were thinking of being in me."

That earned me another growl, and then his hand went to my hair, gripped my bun, his fingers speared deep in my blond locks, as he tilted my head back and kissed me roughly.

My hair, which had been in perfect order, now ruined.

By him.

Praise be.

I arched my breasts into his chest, rough with dark hair, the sensation glorious against my sensitive nipples. He stroked between my legs, pressing a second finger inside me. Taking me to the edge before drawing me back, over and over again. I couldn't withstand this. It had been too long.

Too long since we'd touched. Too long since I'd felt him inside me.

"Hades." I said his name as a plea.

"You will get what you want when I am ready to give it to you," he growled.

I wrapped my hand around his stiff shaft, squeezing him, knowing I could push him to the brink too. I let him take charge because I liked it. Because I enjoyed the feeling of all that strength being used to drive me wild. Because I relished his size, his firm grip.

But I knew full well that if I needed to, I could command his body too.

So I did. Moving my hand from base to tip in slow rhythmic movements until I felt his body begin to shake. He moved away from me for just a moment, returning with a condom that he deftly rolled on before returning to me.

He shoved my panties to the side, then gripping his length, sliding into me slowly. He filled me, made me moan with need before he withdrew and slammed back in hard.

It was rough. It was punishing. It was perfect.

The crescendo to the day.

The release we needed.

We both raced for it, our breathing fractured. We didn't bother to keep quiet.

In the boardroom I had to wear a mask. Here… I was free. Even as he held me fast in his strong arms, I was free.

He whispered things against my mouth. Explicit things that made me shiver. And I cried out with every thrust.

When the wave crashed over us both, he growled and I couldn't hold back a sharp cry, the cascading pleasure almost too much to bear.

After the storm we stayed like that. With me pinned to the wall. Him breathing hard against the crook of my neck. Finally we separated.

"Have you eaten?" he asked.

"No."

"I'll order something."

I nodded and looked around the room at our discarded clothes. This was the landscape of our lives.

Different hotel rooms. The same wreckage.

We never went to each other's homes. The chance for espionage was too great. We didn't…have a relationship. I didn't trust him. I wanted him.

I had wanted him from the very first time I'd met him, with all the limited understanding a girl my age could have for such a thing.

I'd been predisposed to hating him, thanks to his association with his father. Thanks to my own father's feelings on the matter. But I'd seen him and it was like the whole world had slowed down. I'd been fourteen and totally untouched, of course, and yet I'd wanted to know what it was like to kiss him. My fantasies had been fevered then, but romantic more than sexual even as fervent as they were.

By the time I'd been eighteen to his twenty-one, I'd known exactly what I wanted. It was an interesting thing. Our fathers had been rivals and yet they found themselves in the same circles, which meant I'd found myself with Hades. Often.

Back then I'd thought it was love, of course. Even though I'd never had a real conversation with him that hadn't devolved into us being cruel to one another.

That, I'd thought, might be the start of love.

I'd been certain the rush of feeling, the way my heart pounded, had meant something more than animal lust. A virgin's perspective, I realized now. And a protective one at that. Since I'd never wanted to be my mother—who bed-hopped with frequency, and worse, was always engaged in public, messy relationships that ended in court cases and lawsuits for alimony, palimony and child support.

I never wanted to be that.

It was one reason I kept a solid barrier between my desire for Hades and my real life.

Sex, not a relationship.

Sex, not screaming in the streets.

Sex, not headlines.

I didn't let it affect my life outside these rooms. That was how I was different from her. It was why I was successful. A CEO and not a woman who spent her days on a fainting couch in my Lake Como estate paid for by my myriad exes.

Not that I was proud of this. This messy, screwed-up connection we had.

There were reasons we kept it secret beyond my mother being my own personal cautionary tale. Our rivalry was storied in the media. Our companies' competitors. Our personal entanglement would be seen as a conflict of interest, as collusion. It would be…disastrous. Especially for me.

Evidenced by the line of questioning at today's event. What would I do if I lost? What would he do if he won?

I would be absorbed by him. If ever there was a public merger of our…persons, he would be the one who existed, not me. I would be his partner. His lover. My achievements would become his, somehow. I couldn't have it.

Even now that our fathers were dead—or perhaps even more now that our fathers were dead—it had to be secret.

And secret it had been, from the moment I'd slipped him a note with a dry mouth and a pounding heart at a massive charity event on my eighteenth birthday, asking him to meet me in one of the suites.

I'd begged my father for my own room, even though his room had plenty of space. He hadn't questioned me. I wondered sometimes if he'd had an idea that I'd wanted privacy for nefarious reasons, but hadn't minded as long as it hadn't become an issue for him.

That was my dad. He didn't want to know more about me than he had to, because then he might have to contend with something complicated.

That was fine in many ways. I was always grateful to have one parent whose sex life I didn't have to read about in tabloids. I knew too much about my mother. Very little about my father.

Neither of them knew me.

But whatever my father's reasoning, I'd gotten my own suite. And my plan had been set in motion.

Hades had come, his dark eyes glittering. He hadn't trusted me fully even then.

But I'd been thinking about that moment for years. Every time we'd fought, or even looked at each other across a crowded room.

*You know what I want.*

*Do I?*

*Hasn't it been obvious all this time?*

I'd been so afraid he would reject me. Send me away.

Instead, he'd undone the top button on his shirt.

*I know what I want.*

He'd said it as if it was a question. Making sure we were on the same page. We were. Oh, we definitely were.

*I want the same thing. And it's my birthday.*

I'd heard that first times were awkward. That they were painful, messy affairs. Yes, it had hurt right at first when he'd thrust inside me, but there had been nothing awkward about it at all. It had been fire. And so had we.

He had been annoyed with me, though, that I hadn't told him I was a virgin.

I'd tried not to be hurt by it, but I was eighteen

and the man who'd just turned my world on its axis was acting something other than completely thrilled with me.

*Who else would it have been?*

He'd paused then, and looked into my eyes.

Ten years on, Hades looked very different, but that intensity in his dark gaze was the same. He looked at me now as he had then, and maybe that was why he kept me bound to him. Ten years after that first time.

So many times in between I couldn't count them.

A blur of different hotel rooms, different pieces of torn clothing, different curses, promises and dirty words.

"They're bringing you a cheeseburger, *agape*."

My heart hit my breastbone when he returned to me. Those words were hardly poetry, and yet they were.

*Agape*. He called me that. I knew it didn't mean he loved me. I knew it was just a thing he said because it was Greek and exotic and it turned me on.

"Thank you," I said. I realized it was now the time for me to offer to get my own room. "I don't have to stay. I can leave after dinner."

This was a game we played.

He shrugged one shoulder, then went to put his pants on. To deal with the room service, I supposed. "It makes no sense for you to go."

Which meant he wanted more sex. Well, so did I.

I was careful, though, with the blurred lines that existed between myself and Hades. Careful to keep them as unblurred as possible.

"The debate went well," he said. He moved to the bar and picked up a bottle of scotch, pouring a measure for himself.

"Is that on the table to discuss?" I asked.

"We were both there." Meaning there were no potential secrets being traded between us.

"It wasn't a debate, really," I said. "It was meant to be an informative session with the two leading minds in the industry. That's us."

"Mmm." He lifted his glass and drank it all, then poured himself more.

"Are you worried?"

"Me?" He arched a dark brow.

"You're drinking a lot."

He frowned and I knew I'd crossed one of our invisible boundaries. Something like that, acknowledging that over the past ten years of being his dirtiest, secretest secret I might have acquired some intimate knowledge of him, was strictly verboten.

Then it hit me.

"Oh. Hades. It's…it's your father's birthday."

"It isn't. Because he's dead."

"I'm sorry."

"Sorry for what?"

"I don't know, for not acknowledging it sooner?"

He cleared his throat. "And when, Florence, would you have done that? At the event where it was required that we tear strips off each other's flesh? Or here, when I tore strips off your clothes?"

"We don't have an audience here. You can calm down." I moved over to him and stole the glass out of his hand and was gratified when his dark eyes moved over my partially clothed body, the lust there apparent.

"There is nothing to say. He died as he lived. A difficult bastard. You know that."

I did. Our fathers had been brilliant, complex men. I loved my father and I wanted to make him proud, but I had felt the weight of not being the son he wanted keenly. The need to never, ever make a mistake—particularly one that might be perceived as a gender-based mistake—drove me. Like a demon.

It was one reason Hades had always felt both so dangerous and so desirable.

It was a horrible thing to think, but I'd grown up rich, and if I'd ever wanted for anything, it was my father's attention. The truth was, I'd been denied little. But Hades had been off-limits. So I'd never wanted anyone more.

I'd never wanted anyone else at all.

It was his deepest secret, but mine too. If my father had ever known…

Our fathers' rivalry had not been friendly. Not even close. They'd hated each other. I wanted to hate Hades. Part of me did. For all the things he made me feel. But never quite all of me. He drove me insane. I wanted to punch him sometimes. But… I wanted him.

That first time it had been like we were inventing sex. We'd had a four-day event where we were turned loose. We'd had each other everywhere we could find privacy, in every position. I'd gone from novice to experienced very, very quickly, with his hands, his mouth, his body to guide me.

After I'd gone home I'd done my best to accept that it would never happen again. That by the time I saw him next he would have a new woman on his arm and in his bed. And it would be for the best, I knew it. I tried to find a boyfriend. I went on several dates, all ended without so much as a kiss. I couldn't bring myself to want anyone but him.

And when we'd next crossed paths six months later at a scientific symposium in Geneva, I'd expected him to barely acknowledge me. Instead he'd taken me into the nearest single person bathroom and locked the door. He'd had me on a highly polished marble countertop and I'd had no regrets whatsoever about it.

It had taken two years for me to accept that this was how we were.

We were each other's vacation. Each other's outlet. Each other's rebellion. Whenever we met, whatever was happening in his life didn't seem to matter. If he had other girlfriends I didn't ask, didn't want to know. When our paths crossed, that was all there was.

Then his father had died abroad on holiday. I'd been certain that he wouldn't want anything to do with me after that. Now the company was his. Now my father was his direct competition. At the same time, I'd been taking on more and more work for Edison and had been responsible for all the speaking engagements my father would have taken at one time.

We were both speaking at a think tank for the up-and-coming executives in different travel and leisure companies.

We'd been waiting in the same green room, waiting

to be introduced, and he'd reached out and grabbed my bun, tilted my head back and held me steady while he kissed me deep and hard. I'd been dizzy when we'd gone out.

I'd gone back to his room that night. And he had been like a violent storm. He hadn't been like that before. He'd been more like that than not since.

I knew the subject of his father was a tricky one. And we didn't cover tricky subjects. The death of his father felt so…random. He'd been a vital man, even if my father had hated him, I could recognize that. The news had said he'd suffered a medical event and it had seemed a shock to me that such a larger-than-life man could have been taken by something so…common.

Part of me wanted to talk to Hades about it. Comfort him. But that wasn't us. This was dark for him. I could sense the changes in his moods. Hades' moods were like tides. They shifted everything around them. Rearranged the landscape of anyone who got in their path.

It was lucky then, that I'd fashioned my personal landscape into a rock garden a long time ago.

Maybe it was the function of never being quite right for my mother or my father. Maybe it was the necessary result of figuring out how to be what I needed to be to take over Edison, while also being able to smile at the woman who had given birth to me over mimosa brunches. I had a core of steel to make sure that, even as I flexed on the outside, I didn't lose my shape within.

"Perhaps you should dress," Hades said, breaking

through my memories. "Unless you are planning on tipping the delivery person."

"I did not plan to be anywhere near you when the food arrived. I intended to hide under the bed."

The idea that I would be seen with him was ridiculous. And he knew it.

"Of course."

I gathered myself and my clothes and went into the bedroom, where I did not dress.

A few moments later, Hades appeared in the doorway, shirtless, wearing only those dark trousers, holding a tray of food. His dark hair was a mess now, thanks to my hands. His body a perfect testament to the masculine form. Sculpted muscular shoulders; a deep, broad chest; ridged abs.

I could look at him forever and never get tired of it. But looking at him only made me hungry. And not for food.

"You will be upset if you let your food grow cold," he said, pushing away from the doorframe and walking into the room to set the tray at the foot of the bed.

"Who said I was going to let my food get cold?"

"Your expression was asking me for more."

I shrugged, because I knew it would irritate him. "I was looking at the hamburger."

"Of course you were."

It was strange. How I knew this man, but didn't know him. How I liked him sometimes, but didn't. How in some ways he was my longest, closest relationship.

Perhaps that spoke to a measure of loneliness in my life. Or maybe I was lonely in part because of him.

I had a friend, Sarah, who worked at Edison, though there was…

I couldn't help but feel it was my fault that I wasn't as close to Sarah as I wanted to be. Because nobody knew about Hades. Nobody. I had never told another living soul.

I had made up mystery lovers. Because there were a couple of times that Sarah and I had been on the same business trip, and I'd disappeared overnight. So what could be said? I had fashioned a lie that made me sound maybe more adventurous than I was. I acted as if it was never the same man.

Of course it was. Distressingly, always the same man.

And with this man, there was only ever one way it could be.

I had imagined conversations with Sarah about it in my head before.

"And what is your plan?" Fake Sarah would ask. "To be with him like this forever? Until you both die alone and are buried with this secret?"

"I was thinking so," I would reply.

And in my imagination, my friend did not tell me that was ridiculous and sad.

There was of course, always the possibility that I would meet a man who made me feel half of what Hades did, but who made up for that by filling the other half with care, attention, soft feelings. Romantic feelings.

Not this hard and sharp need that made us both lose control at every opportunity.

I didn't need that. Not forever. It was just that I had never even met a man who made me feel half.

I could give this up. Someday. But surely half wasn't too much to ask.

I stretched across the bed and grabbed my plate.

"When will you next be in the city?" I asked the question casually, because he often worked in Europe, but the time he spent in New York was one of the few times we were able to meet up when we weren't at a special event. And maybe, sometimes, I found excuses to go and work in the London office of Edison so that it was convenient for us to meet up there.

A couple of times a year. But that was all.

"I will be there for the next month," he said.

The words hit me low. Hard. A month?

I imagined that. Going to his temporary residence more nights than not. Gorging myself on him. We never had that kind of time.

It would dovetail into the Christmas season and everything would be decked out. It would almost be… romantic. But we weren't romantic.

Undoubtedly he would be busy, but our toxic trait—one of the many, really—was that we always made time for sex. Even if it was just an hour of time, we would find a way.

I'd once met him on the tarmac when we'd been in the same city for an hour while his plane refueled and he'd taken me in the luxury bedroom on board. Then I'd deplaned trying to look like we'd been having a meeting.

Our level of determination and opportunism combined with that length of time was… Dizzying.

"I'll call you," he said.

"You will not," I said. "You'll text me an address."

He chuckled. "You never know if the media is listening in on phone calls."

"Not mine. They know that I'm terribly boring."

I took a French fry off my plate and reclined against the pillow, giving him a full view of my naked body.

"Terribly boring," he repeated. There was something strange in his expression. I couldn't read it. But then, when it came to feelings, I could never quite read him.

"Finish eating," he said. "I want my dessert."

That expression I could read.

Familiar and thrilling. My darkest secret.

One I was happy to keep forever.

# CHAPTER THREE

He hadn't texted. It was fine.

That night in DC had been…

I still felt wrecked by it. I couldn't quite explain it.

Maybe it was the intensity I felt over the event. Over that undecided contract. Or maybe it was him. The fact that it had been his father's birthday.

Either way, there had been something different in the way we came together each time that night. We had used the chaise and the bed in the exact ways I'd known we would, but there had been a layer to it all that was…it was just different. I couldn't pinpoint it. When I'd woken up in the morning, he was gone.

Not unprecedented, but it had felt strange and wrong after everything.

I didn't know why.

It wasn't different.

It was us.

Maybe I was romanticizing.

That thought brought me up short as I pushed away from my desk and moved to the corner of the office. It was all windows, looking down over the Upper East Side. Beautiful.

I loved the city. Though, I loved London equally. I had dual citizenship, courtesy of my mother, who was an alarmingly excessive London socialite who had children with billionaires as if it had been her retirement plan. She worked. But not in a corporate sense. Her job was to be beautiful, engaging, *decorative*.

She did it well.

Consequently, I had an older half brother who was an Italian count, and one who owned Andalusians in Spain. They probably knew Hades. Those sorts of men, brooding and preposterous, typically flocked together.

Maybe they entertained socialites on their yachts.

That was the thing that wealthy men could do, which I could never be caught dead doing.

I bit the inside of my cheek. I did not like to think about Hades with other women. But we never spoke about that. I didn't own his body, whatever I might feel.

And for me… There had never been anyone else.

But I knew that I had benefited greatly from previously established skill the first time we were together. He had been no virgin. Anyway, he had been twenty-one years old. I had no reason to believe he had been anything like faithful to me in the years since.

Faithful?

Faithfulness implied the presence of a relationship. Which we definitely did not have.

I knew that. So the question of why I was preoccupied with Hades while at work was one I should probably sit down and answer. Maybe I should get my bullet journal and make some goals.

*Do not think about sexy business rival while trying to get work done.*

That seemed like a pretty basic skill that was really logical for anyone who wanted to succeed in business.

I looked at my phone, in spite of myself. There was still no text from Hades.

But there was one from Sarah.

Coming up. Crazy news.

I instantly Googled my name. Which was maybe a weird response to that, but of course when she said there was crazy news, I was instantly concerned that it was about me. Had somebody seen Hades and me at the same hotel in Washington DC? Of course, their go-to assumption would not be that we had been sleeping together. I didn't think.

I scrolled through endlessly regurgitated articles that popped up when I tried to filter the most recent entries first. None of it seemed to be real news. Just listicles about the best red lipstick worn by powerful women, and my best black suits.

Flattering. I had to admit. But not exactly crazy news.

The door to my office opened, and Sarah thrust her phone into my face.

"What am I looking at?" I asked.

"He's engaged."

"Who?"

"Hades."

The room tilted, but I could feel my face freeze. No reaction. My chest felt cold. She couldn't be right. I had slept with the man three days ago. He hadn't mentioned a fiancée. He was frequently in the news, but hadn't been photographed with anyone. It was impossible.

I couldn't say all of that.

So I just made a weird, inarticulate noise and took the phone from her hand.

*Billionaire Hades Achelleos set to wed heiress Jessica Lane in lavish London ceremony.*

"I… I don't understand."

"I wouldn't have expected it," Sarah said. "The man seems like he has ice chips in his veins."

"It's just… It can't be true. The timing is…" She could feel Sarah staring at her. "What I mean is, we are in the middle of competing for this NASA contract. Why would he plan a wedding during that? It seems silly. It seems like he's just handing me the win."

"That is true," said Sarah.

I was going to be sick. I was literally in danger of vomiting on the carpet. He was getting married.

He was getting married.

That bastard was getting married, and he hadn't even had the common courtesy to tell me?

He wasn't mine. He never had been. I knew that. I had known this whole time. Okay, maybe I hadn't known it at first. But I had tried to tell myself that. I had made an attempt to be sure that I kept my feelings disengaged from the whole thing. He wasn't a prop, he was a human being, so sometimes I might feel things, but that was to be expected. Because I wasn't a sociopath. But I was…

I sat down in my chair. Was I the other woman?

Was he in love with somebody else, or at least pretending to be, this woman who probably loved him, and he was cheating on her, with me?

That had never occurred to me. I had imagined him perhaps entertaining vapid socialites on his yacht. I had not imagined that… Did he live with her?

"Are you okay?"

I looked up at Sarah. I honestly didn't know what to say. Except I had to find something. Something that wasn't the truth. "I'm just shocked."

I knew that I was acting like a weird robot. But it was that or cry, and confess that I had a terrible secret that it was especially important nobody knew.

The idea of what that would do to my reputation…

They would make me out to be some kind of barracuda. Someone who was sleeping with the competition in order to… I don't know…steal secrets from him? Engage in corporate espionage? Ruin his life? It would be unflattering.

I knew that, because I knew how the media wrote about women. I had seen them do it to my own mother, time and time again. Granted, it wasn't exactly a fabrication when they wrote those things about my mother. But I already knew that I would be tarred with the same brush. Easily. Quickly.

I trusted Sarah. But I could not bring myself to

speak about what happened between Hades and myself out loud. Just the idea of it filled my mouth with a metallic tang.

"He is… He is the most vile man that I have ever met, and I hope that woman doesn't sign a prenup. I hope that when they divorce, and they will, she'll get everything. And I really hope they don't have children."

"Wow," said Sarah.

"You don't understand," I said, rage beginning to flood my chest. "He is… He is the single most vile human being that I have ever had the misfortune of knowing."

"You used *vile* twice."

"Well, it fits."

I pushed up from my chair and I began to pace the room. I couldn't sit still anymore. I was electrified with outrage. And thank God for it. It was saving me from the very real threat of shedding tears, which I refused to do.

"He would be a terrible father," I said.

The words fell out of my mouth like lead bullets.

"I actually thought you would find this funny," said Sarah. "The very idea of the man engaging in something quite as traditional as the institution of marriage."

"It isn't funny," I said. "Because she's a real woman. She's a real woman who has been… Tricked by him."

"You don't know that. She is a socialite. It's entirely possible that this is something of a marriage of convenience."

But what if it wasn't? What if she loved him. And he had spent last Thursday with me tied to a bed.

I told myself that was why I was upset. It certainly wasn't because he was stopping things with me without saying a single word.

Why would he? He didn't owe me anything.

That was my official stance.

"I have work to do," I said.

"Okay," said Sarah, frowning.

"See you later."

"You were just with him, weren't you?"

I looked up. Sarah was gazing at me now with no small amount of questions in her eyes.

"I wasn't with him," I said. "We just saw each other at the NASA event. Which you know already."

"Yes. You're right. I do. I'm going to call you later, Florence."

Sarah left me then, to my dark thoughts, which were teeming around inside of me like tussling eels. I tried to work for an hour. And then I did something… That I never did. I called my driver, and I gave him the address of Hades' office.

The entire drive there was a blur. I wasn't being discreet. But it was fine. I was allowed to go to his office. After all, we were business rivals. There were occasions when we might have to speak.

I walked into the office building, and the woman at the desk looked at me wide-eyed. "Ms. Clare," she said.

"Hi, yes," I said, trying to sound official. "I have a meeting with Mr. Achelleos."

"I don't have you written down."

"He'll see me," I said.

Because of who I was she let me in. Let me go up to the top floor. Elevators. I was always waiting in elevators, and that didn't really bother me normally. They were my safe private space to expel the energy that I couldn't risk letting out in public. But I didn't want to let any of it out in here. I wanted to unleash all of it on him.

The elevator doors opened and I got halfway down the hall toward his office before I realized I wasn't exactly sure what I was coming here to do.

It didn't matter, though, because once I set my mind to something, I was certain about it. I couldn't afford to be anything else.

I walked into the room without knocking. He was standing at the window, facing away from me. "You should know better than to come here."

He didn't turn. Of course, the secretary had let him know that I was on my way up. But he hadn't locked the door. I did, because I didn't want anyone walking in on this discussion.

He turned toward me, and he had the nerve to look perfect. His dark hair swept back perfectly, his suit tailored perfectly. He looked well rested. He looked like a man who was on top of his game in every way. A man whose life was going exactly how he wanted it to.

I hated him then. More than I ever had.

"How dare you?"

"I'm sorry, what do I dare today?"

"Do not play dumb, Hades. It doesn't suit you. You're many things, but you're not dumb. You must know the news of your impending nuptials broke today."

He waved his hand. "Oh. That."

"That?" I was speechless. Which never happened to me.

"Yes. What of it?"

"You didn't tell me."

"How is it relevant to you? When have we ever updated one another on changes in our personal lives."

"You might have told me that Washington DC was the last time. I asked when I was going to see you."

Well. I should have actually planned a speech, because I hated everything that came out of my mouth just then. Because it sounded hurt more than angry. And hurt on my own behalf, and not poor Jessica Lane's, who was marrying a bastard that had been cheating on her. Which was what I was supposed to be mad about. His making me the other woman against my will.

"I don't know why it has to be the last time," he said.

"What… Planet to do you live on?"

"As far as you and I go, my marriage changes nothing."

He really believed that. He really… He really thought that the wedding was nothing. Like getting a wife was like getting a pair of new shoes. That it had nothing to do with me because the encounters we had were so separate from his actual life. Because I was so separate from his actual life.

I knew that he didn't love me. I had never claimed to love him. Not since I was a virginal teenage girl. And even then, I had only ever claimed it in my diary.

Right now I was definitely acting like a woman scorned. It was one thing, though, to know we weren't in love. I never thought we were. It was another to realize what little regard he held me in. He didn't see me as a person. While I had at least seen him as my equal, as my nemesis, he had seen me as a plaything.

Of all things, that had never occurred to me.

"I hate you," I said. "I hate you and I never want to see you again."

"You came to my office, *agape*. If you did not wish to see me, that was perhaps a bad first move."

I found myself striding across the space, without even thinking. I walked up to him and I shoved at his shoulder.

He caught my wrist and pulled me forward. My stomach twisted.

I knew. I knew how this would end.

The way that it always did.

"After this, I don't want to see you. We will no longer conduct meetings in the same space. We will contend with NASA in a different way."

"Fine by me," he said. After this. Because we both knew.

Perhaps that was why DC had been so intense. He had known. But I hadn't. I deserved this. I deserved the chance to make him feel what I felt. To pour all of my intensity out onto him.

I deserved this chance to know that this was the last time.

I wrenched the knot on his tie and flung it down to the ground. I tore his jacket off his shoulders, and then his shirt, violently. I made sure it lost buttons. I made sure that he couldn't simply put the shirt back on like I had never been here. I would not let him walk away from this unruffled. Because nothing had ever made me angrier than when I walked in to see him looking as beautiful and unstained as ever, as if he hadn't just unleashed news upon the world that rocked me to my steel core.

But he was no kinder to me. He ripped my blouse away from my body, and my bra, leaving me nothing but my pencil skirt, which he unzipped, so hard I thought he had torn the zipper down through the seam.

Maybe he had.

Right then, I didn't care. My eyes burned with tears, but I refused to shed them. I refused to show any emotion. Other than anger.

The color mounted in his cheeks, his need apparent. I slipped his belt out from the loops, and he took it from me, gripped my wrists and lifted them up over my head, and before I could react, he slipped the end of the belt through the buckle and tightened it fast around me, binding my hands. I was too shocked to protest, and when he laid me down across the clear edge of his massive corner desk, he pushed my arms up above my head, his expression one of pure, violent need.

"I bet you can't do this with her," I said.

A betrayal. Of my jealousy.

I was jealous. I didn't care about her. I didn't care if I was the other woman. I cared that I had been wounded. I cared that I could no longer deny that he had been with other women. I cared that perhaps I was not singular to him in the way he was to me.

I cared.

I cared.

I cared.

And I hated him for it.

He didn't respond to me, not with anything other than a growl. But he tore the skirt away from my body, leaving me in my thigh-high stockings and black high heels.

He took the rest of his clothes off and came back to me, moving his hand to my throat as he kissed me, hard and deep. I wanted to touch him, but he held my hands down still.

He held me fast as he thrust deep inside of me, looked into my eyes as he claimed me, over and over again. I took my bound hands and lifted them up over his head, as his hold tightened on my neck, I held my arms around him, locked together as he took me.

I took him back.

Because I would be certain of one thing.

That he would not forget this. That he would not forget me.

That he would regret the day that he had chosen

to take half of what we shared in exchange for that bland, ordinary life. The one I had told myself I might take someday.

He had made the bargain before I did.

And it called to me. Wounded me.

I struggled against his hold, arched my neck upward and bit him, at the side of his throat. Hard enough that I left a dark mark behind.

His lip curled, and he looked feral then. As he went over the edge, and his own loss of control spurred mine.

We cried out, together. Uncaring if anyone heard.

We had wrecked this place. And each other.

For the last time.

For ten years this had been the landscape of my life.

The landscape of us.

It was over now. There was no more us.

He exhaled, hard, then pulled the belt back through the loop, freeing me, freeing himself. He stepped away from me and wordlessly went to collect his clothes.

I had a difficult time doing the same. My skirt was ruined, my shirt was too. I tucked the blouse in as tightly as I could, crossing the edges together. It would be good enough to get me to my car. Especially with my black jacket over the top of it.

It was a mundane thought.

But mundane thoughts were the only things that were going to get me out of this building without having a total mental breakdown.

I didn't say goodbye to him.

I didn't say anything.

I'd said all I needed to with my body.

And when I was finally in the back of the car, I put up the barrier between myself and my driver. And I wept.

# CHAPTER FOUR

THE TROUBLE WAS my daily life didn't change after that last time. I went to work. I went home. I went out for drinks with Sarah. I called my mother and listened to her talk about the party she was putting together. She complained that my half brother Rocco wouldn't come with his new wife. She wanted him to add some class to the place.

I laughed.

My mum was often hilariously self-aware. It was no mystery why she'd managed to wrap so many men around her finger. While the press printed truths about her, they were half-truths. No one would believe she was funny, clever and very dry, because the press made her out to be nothing more than a vacuous socialite. She was a vacuous socialite. She was just also funny, clever and dry.

All of this, though, made it so hard for me to remember some days that my life had changed forever two weeks earlier.

I'd ended things with him.

We weren't between assignations. We were done.

I would forget sometimes. Then news about his

wedding would be on my home page. Jessica Lane was apparently a very popular social media girlie. Which meant every choice she made, from venue to dress to stemware was much discussed.

I hated her.

It wasn't fair.

It was bad feminism.

I didn't care. But I didn't care in the privacy of my own head. Because the consequence of carrying on a secret affair for ten years was that the heartbreak was also secret. My own private hell. Just for me. Hooray.

Maybe what made me hate her most was that she got to be online in ruffles and pastels, with pink lipstick and softness. She got to be feminine and soft in a way I never felt I was allowed to be. When I was with Hades we weren't pastel. We were bold. Vivid. Sharp. Painful.

Maybe he'd needed soft.

I was so tired of myself.

I flew to Houston for another NASA meeting. Then I went to Cape Canaveral for the next. I didn't see him there. I'd made sure I wouldn't.

I went back to my hotel room after the meetings and stretched across the white bedspread with my arms out like I was making a miserable snow angel.

I went back and dived into work like it was my salvation.

He won the contract.

I watched his live stream about it in spite of myself, and then I took my phone and threw it so hard across the room that it cracked against the marble kitchen countertop.

I sat on the floor with my head in my hands, and for the first time I really contemplated the concept of failure.

*Clare Heir Can't Hack It.*

*Florence Clare, Discarded by Hades Achelleos and NASA in the Same Month!*

I could only give thanks the press couldn't actually write that headline. First of all, because no one knew about Hades and myself, and second of all because I'd discarded him.

*It changes nothing...*

How dare he?

I decided I needed a break. I called Sarah. "Do you want to work remotely for a few weeks?"

"Where?"

"Lake Como?"

Sarah laughed. "Are you kidding?"

"No. I'm not kidding. My mother has a house there."

"Well, yes, that would be amazing. You…you want to go stay with your mother?"

I did. Which was weird. I loved my mother, but I loved her with a bit of distance. The idea of being swept up into her sphere felt… It felt like a potential rescue.

Knowing Mom, there would be oiled-up men running around anyway. If I wanted to have a revenge lay, I could certainly find one. That made me feel ghastly.

"She's having a party. It will be fun. Also her house

is so big it's more like staying in the same town than the same residence. We won't even see her every day."

I hadn't asked her yet, but as soon as Sarah agreed, I called.

"Mom, would you mind if a friend and I came to stay for a while?"

"Ooh, a friend, Flo?"

I grimaced. "No. Not like that. She is my actual friend."

It made me think of Hades. We'd never been friends.

I stared out my apartment windows, down at all the lights below. I couldn't remember why I loved the city.

I didn't tell my mother I'd lost the contract—she wouldn't have any idea I'd been competing for one. She saw the success of the company, that I had status, and that was really—not all she cared about—but it spoke of success to her so the details didn't matter.

The next day I overpacked everything floaty and feminine that I owned. I packed makeup I never wore and face creams I forgot to apply, and Sarah and I took the private corporate jet to Italy.

The flight attendant offered champagne but I didn't have the stomach for it. I didn't have the stomach for much of anything.

"It's all going to work out," Sarah said, gently as we descended.

"I don't see how."

I said that before I realized she meant for the company. After not getting the contract. Because she didn't know about Hades.

Both felt equally hopeless to me.

"What if it doesn't?" I asked. "I always thought it would if I just figured out how to be enough. But I haven't."

"It was one contract, Florence. It isn't the end of anything. You didn't need it to keep the company financially solvent."

"It feels like the end," I said.

I couldn't explain it. Not because I didn't have the words. Because I genuinely couldn't explain it.

I was temporarily distracted from my misery by the beauty of Lake Como. Apparently even in the depths of this…this despair that was entirely foreign to me, I could still pause to appreciate the beauty of Italy. I was glad of that. Maybe I wasn't going to need to see a therapist after all.

It shouldn't be like this. The end of whatever we had.

It was the contract on top of it. I knew that. Perhaps, it was even the bigger issue. It had to be. Because I was acting like my heart had been broken by someone I was in love with. I had been foolish in a whole lot of different ways when it came to Hades. But I wasn't that foolish.

My mother's house on the lake was gorgeous. The crowning achievement of one of her divorces.

She often said that, then laughed and said she supposed she would actually have to give that title to Rocco. He was her son, after all.

The house was a stunning yellow, with broad stone

decks that extended out from the hill where it sat nestled over the lake.

When we arrived, my mother sent staff. She was on her way out to dinner and too busy to chat overmuch. She floated through like a butterfly, kissed my cheek and met Sarah enthusiastically. Then she was gone.

Her staff graciously allowed Sarah and I to take over a quadrant at one end of the house, and we were able to establish office space as well as our own bedrooms. I kept all of my focus on the company's internal network. I did not look at the broader internet. I refused to check any progress on Hades' upcoming wedding. I told myself that I definitely didn't know how many days away it was every time I woke up.

But I also did my best to ignore how increasingly tired and awful I felt every morning.

Because it felt like a weakness.

Not only had I failed, but I was allowing that failure to change me.

We were sitting out on the terrace one glorious morning, with a massive spread of food in front of us, jams and cream, croissants. Espresso, lattes and sipping chocolate. Cured meats, a selection of cheeses and olives. Because my mother did not care what time of day it was. It was always time for a charcuterie in her opinion.

One of the things I enjoyed about her.

"You seem heartbroken," she said, leaning back in her chair, wearing large sunglasses that covered half of her face.

Sarah had taken an instant liking to my mother,

which was handy. Though I think my mother interpreted Sarah's desire to speak with her as frequently as possible as admiration, and I suspected Sarah was fascinated by her, like a specimen she was examining for research purposes.

Which was fair enough. My mother was eminently examinable.

"It's the contract," Sarah said. "Florence loves the company more than she loves anything."

"Flo needs to get more of a personal life," my mother said.

"Florence is sitting right here," I said. "Why did you name me Florence if you insist on shortening it."

"Your father named you," she said. "I wanted to name you Trixie."

Well. Then I never would've been CEO.

"It's the contract," I said.

My mother lowered her sunglasses. She was supernaturally smooth, her lips extending beyond the boundary of their natural line thanks to years of fillers. She was a beautiful woman, my mother, though natural beauty was not, and had never been, her priority. She made me feel dull. I could tell myself that I found her to be gaudy and over-the-top, but it didn't change the fact that next to her I felt like a pale, less vibrant photocopy.

"No," my mother said. "It is not the contract."

"It is," I insisted, standing up and grabbing a plate, determined to fill it. Determined to stop acting like I was heartbroken, because it was stupid.

Hades' wedding was tomorrow. That was just fine,

and I wasn't thinking about it, because I wasn't looking at the news.

Just then, one of my mother's staff came out with a tray of pastries to add to the collection, along with a stack of newspapers.

I reached out and grabbed a piece of cheese off my plate and bit into it. Just as my mother grabbed hold of the newspaper and set it down on the table. And there it was. Front-page news on her favorite scandal sheet.

*Achelleos Nuptials More Expensive Than Two Royal Weddings Combined!*

Just then, the cheese that I was attempting to swallow decided it wasn't going down without a fight. My stomach lurched, and I ran from the balcony, stumbling into the nearest bathroom—thankfully they were all over the house—and found myself falling to my knees in front of the actual gold toilet. Where I did indeed lose the battle with the cheese.

I sat there for a moment, completely humiliated.

Hopefully no one had guessed what had made me react that way.

Maybe I could claim exhaustion. Overwork. A stomach bug.

Anything other than a headline about my supposed enemy's wedding.

I stood up and splashed water on my face before walking back out to the terrace, trying to look like I was fine. I was not fine.

Sarah looked worried. My mother had a small smile on her face.

"Oh, finally, Flo. I can see that you're my daughter."

"What?"

"You're like me after all!"

"In what way? Lactose intolerant?"

She laughed. "No. You've made a bad decision, haven't you?"

If only it was *one* bad decision. If only. It was so many bad decisions so many different times over the course of so many years. And I had convinced myself that by partitioning them off, separating them into a different part of my life, that I wouldn't be affected by them. Not seriously.

I had been in denial all this time.

Because the decisions that I had made in private could no longer be contained behind the door.

They were bursting through into the regular part of my life, and it was just so terrible.

"I'm just not very well."

"You're not pregnant?"

I froze.

"No," I said.

Sarah was staring at me now, and it wasn't concern on her face exclusively anymore. It was curiosity.

"I can't be pregnant," I said.

"Like you don't think you're pregnant? Or you *can't* be pregnant," Sarah asked. "Because those are two different things."

"It's…"

I was beginning to feel dizzy again. I closed my eyes.

"I *can't be*," I said.

Because there was nothing worse, nothing worse

in the entire world that I could think of happening at this moment.

But I couldn't ignore the evidence that was flooding into my mind now. Very logical things that I had been ignoring for a good long while.

My period was late.

I was exhausted.

I was emotional.

I was nauseous in the morning.

I had just vomited up a piece of cheese like it was poison.

Most damning of all, I knew full well that we had not used protection in his office. I had wanted to think about it, I had wanted to acknowledge it. The entire encounter had been so painful that I hadn't wanted to play it over in my head. But I knew that he hadn't used a condom. I hadn't been aware of it so much right at the time. I wouldn't have remembered it then if a giant neon sign had flashed on reminding me to have safe sex. Later, when I'd started to try and gather myself again at home, it had become apparent to me.

But I pushed it to the side. Like I had pushed all of it to the side.

He and I were usually so careful. We couldn't afford to be anything else.

But we hadn't been careful that day. We had been dangerous.

"Oh, Florence," said Sarah, wincing. "You *are* pregnant, aren't you?"

"Is he rich?" This was of course my mother's first question.

That snapped me out of my momentary catatonia.

"That doesn't matter," I said. "*I'm* already rich."

"So was I," said my mother, waving her hand. "I wasn't estate in Lake Como rich, though. And now I am."

"Money is not my concern," I said.

I sat there for a long moment. And I tried to decide what I was going to do.

There was no use denying it, not to myself or anyone. As much as I wanted to.

It wasn't only my mum and Sarah I had to face. It wasn't only the board of the company and the public.

If I appeared suddenly, pregnant, *he* was going to know. Unless he could somehow be convinced that it was a rebound… Unless I could make him believe that I'd always had other lovers, and maybe I didn't even know who the baby belonged to. He wouldn't believe it. That was the problem. On some level, I was convinced that he had always known the degree to which he had me ensnared.

Also, he would be well aware at this point that he hadn't used a condom with me. The timing would be far too coincidental, he would make inquiries and demands about it. He was that sort of man.

But I couldn't wait until after he was married.

I really was trying to not care about his fiancée. After I had embraced my own selfishness, after I had decided to make love with him one last time, I thought it seemed a little bit hypocritical. But she should know. Before she married him, she needed to know that he was expecting a baby with another woman.

It was entirely possible Hades would want nothing to do with the child. Except…

I thought of the way he looked whenever the subject of his father came up. I thought of the way it affected him. And somehow, I knew the subject of children would be a thorny one, but also one he would not shy away from, because he was not a man to shy away from anything.

I couldn't hide it. Eventually, the media would find out, and they would take control of the story. We had a very short space of time where we could control the narrative. If he wanted to give up parental rights, to give up any claim on the baby, then I could simply say that it was artificial insemination and I had chosen to have a baby by myself.

That would be a great story. One that would make me sound like I was taking control of my life.

I did not let myself think about what a baby that belonged to both me and Hades would look like. I didn't let myself imagine a little boy with his dark eyes or little girl with glossy black hair.

No. I couldn't be sentimental about this. There was no sentiment. He was marrying somebody else. He didn't care about me. But everything would have to be entirely clear, entirely out in the open between us before it became public fodder.

That much I knew.

"I have to go. Right now."

"Why?" Sarah asked. "You could see a doctor, you could get a test…"

“We’ll get one when we get back to New York. We don’t have any time to waste.”

“Why?” Sarah asked.

“Because we have to get there before the wedding.”

# CHAPTER FIVE

Leaving Lake Como was interesting. Given I was losing my mind, and Sarah had forced the driver to stop in a minute market on our way to the airport to get a pregnancy test.

"You have to know," she said.

But I already did. It was like the veil had been lifted and I just couldn't deny the truth anymore. That's what I'd been doing. For weeks. Denying. Ignoring. I was so good at that, because in my position I'd had to be.

She had me take the test as soon as we reached altitude.

I knew she was mad at me. Because obviously I had been keeping a huge secret from her. But…

"Sarah…"

"Take the test, and then we'll talk. No. We'll make a strategy. I'm going to get out the Post-it notes."

"We don't need Post-it notes."

"We need Post-it notes and Washi tape, Florence. There is no other option."

I went into the bathroom as instructed. I didn't usually do what I was told. In fact, I was more or less allergic to it. But right now I didn't feel like I was in any position to argue. Right now, it kind of felt good for someone to just give me some instructions.

Of course, waiting for the test did not feel good. And watching that second pink line begin to materialize was…

I knew. At that point I absolutely knew, but still, seeing it like that…

I practically ran out of the bathroom. "It's positive. I knew it. We didn't actually need to stop for the test and…"

"He's probably going to want to know there was a test," she said.

I sighed. "You say that like you know him."

"I know his type. I don't know him, because I didn't actually think we were supposed to do any fraternizing with the enemy. Do you want to… Speak to that?"

"It happened after I found out about the engagement," I said.

She just kept staring at me, and I knew it was an insufficient explanation. I waited a moment. To just be very sure that she needed me to actually explain. That she needed me to tell her the whole story. Everything. Apparently she did.

"Because… It wasn't the first time."

"Oh, Florence," she said, pressing her finger to her forehead. "He was at every one of those conferences where you disappeared."

"How long have you suspected?" I asked.

"It occurred to me a couple of times that maybe… It's only that sometimes you get this look on your face when you see him. And it isn't entirely bloodthirsty. It is a little bloodthirsty, it just isn't only bloodthirsty."

"I never wanted anyone to know."

"I'm your friend."

"It's been going on for longer than I've known you," I said.

She threw her hands up in the air and sat there frozen, her expression one of near-comedic shock. Except nothing was funny.

"I seduced him on my eighteenth birthday," I said.

"*No*," she said.

"Yes. And ever since then… It just happens. It just happens. In cities all over the world, in different hotel rooms. In bathrooms, sometimes. Once a library at an English manor."

I had forgotten about that. Well. I had deliberately chosen not to think about that, because it had been one of the more lovely and romantic times. There had been an edge of danger to it. Because we had sneaked away from a party, and even though the doors were locked, he hadn't been fast, and I had been worried we would be missed.

He spread me out on the rug in front of the fireplace. He looked at me like I was special.

Or it had been a trick of the light. Because I had clearly never been special.

"So you have been having a secret relationship with your chief competition since before you were actually CEO of the company."

"It isn't a relationship," I said.

"When you saw that he was engaged, you looked like you were going to be sick."

"Because he slept with me when he was with her. I didn't know about that. I didn't know about her. I would never..."

That was a lie. Because I had.

"I can't forgive him for that," I said.

"No. Are you going to stop the wedding?"

"No. But I think that she needs to know. He also needs to know, but she really needs to know. Don't you think?"

"Yes," Sarah said slowly. "I think I would want to know."

"Well, that's what I think. Before she actually makes vows to him, she should know. Because this baby was conceived after their engagement." I stared out the window. "Their engagement was announced just a little over a month ago. You realize that means they were together for a very long time before that."

Sarah nodded. "Yes."

"I can't just let that stand."

"Are you motivated by justice? Or revenge?"

I shifted uncomfortably. "Does it matter?"

"Not really," she said.

Because she knew, I finally started talking about it. About the years of it. About how sometimes I convinced myself that having him after one of our big showdowns was my reward.

About how I tried to present myself as this very serious, very successful businesswoman, but I was as distracted by men as anybody. By one man.

"He's hot," said Sarah. "I just thought that you were…" She looked almost disappointed, and I hated that. "I thought you were as bulletproof as you pretended to be."

"Sadly," I said. "I'm not immune to all bullets."

We landed in New York, and the wedding was only ninety minutes away.

I texted him. In desperation. He didn't answer.

I went to his apartment. He wasn't there. I did not want to go to the church, but I was starting to see no other option.

"You want me to wait for you?" Sarah asked.

"I might need you to run interference."

Sarah nodded. "Whatever you need."

We got out of the car, and while we were dressed fairly nicely, we had just been on Lake Como on vacation, and I had brought pretty clothes, we weren't really dressed for a wedding that cost two times a royal wedding. I also wasn't dressed anything like I normally did. My hair was a mess, loose, and I was wearing pink. I also looked like I felt like garbage.

Only because I did feel like garbage.

So that was nice.

We ran up the steps to the big, stone church, only to be met by security.

"I'm Florence Clare," I said. "I'm obviously invited to the wedding."

He looked at me. "I don't have your name on any list."

"That is a mistake," I said. "Hades and I have a business relationship."

Sarah looked at me. I refused to look back.

"I don't have your name on the list," said the security guard. But he wasn't even looking.

"You just know that," I said.

"I know who you are, Ms. Clare," he said. "If you were invited to the wedding, I would have remembered seeing your name."

"It was an oversight." I opened up my phone and showed him that the last text I had sent was to Hades. Showing him that I had Hades' personal number made me sweaty.

"I'll go inside and just check with his secretary," he said.

"You do that," I said.

He walked into the church, and Sarah caught the door.

"Go," she said.

Without thinking, I skittered inside behind the security guard and dodged into a hallway out of his view. My heart was pounding. I felt like I was going to throw up again. I could not be skulking around the church where Hades was getting married and vomiting.

So I did my best to gather my courage, and I tried to figure out where he could be. I looked at the text again. Nothing from him. But suddenly one from Sarah came through.

It was a picture of the church's layout that she must have gotten from online.

She had circled two rooms that she clearly thought might be used for people getting ready.

I tried to orient myself.

Another text from her came in.

I'm going to tell the guard you weren't well and you left. I won't go far.

Thanks.

I made my way down the hall and tried to follow the map.

The building was old, and my steps echoed so loudly, in time with my heartbeat. I was sure that I was alerting everyone within a fifty-foot radius to my presence. I tried to move more softly, even as I kept my pace quick.

I peered into a window on the first door, and it was a room full of people preparing flowers. Definitely not Hades.

I made my way to the next room and saw that the window was blocked. The door opened suddenly, swinging out toward me, and I moved back.

"Are you one of the florists?" a beautiful, brown-skinned woman wearing a bright pink dress asked.

"Yes," I said.

"Okay. Do you have Jessica's okay?"

"Not quite yet. They're still putting the finishing touches on it. But will bring it down in a minute."

"Great," she said. Obviously the maid of honor. Thankfully, the wedding colors looked like they were pink, so I looked like I belonged here. And I wasn't especially recognizable with my hair down, and without my signature black.

The door closed again, and I stood there for a moment, wondering if I should just talk to Jessica first. No.

I did think she should know, but Hades was the father of the baby. He needed to know first.

I had no idea where to go next, though.

I looked back on the schematic and saw that there was an outdoor grotto in the middle of the church. I wove through the core door, looking for it.

I didn't know why, but for some reason I just thought that I might find him there. Just maybe.

There was a big wooden door with no window, but from the looks of the map, it was the door that led outside. I opened it up, and there he was. Standing with his back to me, the way he had been when I had come to confront him at his office.

And just like then, he straightened, as if he could feel me.

*You silly girl, it's any person walking up behind him. It has nothing to do with you specifically.*

He turned around, and our eyes clashed. For a brief moment, it felt like I was falling through the earth. It felt like the world had fallen away, and there was nothing. Not the earth, not the sky, not gravity. Only him. Only me.

"Florence," he said.

For some reason, hearing my name on his lips made tears spring to my eyes. It made me angry.

"I'm not here to stop your wedding," I said.

I refused to allow him to think, even for a moment, that I was so weak for him, that I would do something that silly.

"Of course not," he said.

"I'm just here…"

He crossed the space between us and grabbed the back of my head. His kiss was a shock. Cruel and hard. It was angry. And I found myself surrendering to him helplessly.

Even as my better self stood by and watched in horror as my weak self succumbed to his touch. I had no practice doing anything else when it came to Hades.

None at all.

He was my one and only.

He was the father of my baby.

That thought gave me the strength to pull away.

"I know what you came for," he said.

"I didn't come for that either," I said. "You don't know me, Hades. Even if you think that you do."

"I've been your lover for a decade, *agape*. Don't tell me that I don't know you. I know every sigh, every scream, I know the way that your blue eyes darken when you need me. I know just how dark your fantasies are. How the cold, calculated businesswoman likes for someone to tell her what to do as long as she's naked. How you wish for someone to tie you down and make your decisions for you. I don't just know what you want, Florence. I know what you beg for."

He made my knees weak. But while I had been weak with him for all of these years, I wouldn't be weak now. There was too much at stake. I was in shock, and I had had very little time to process any of this, so the part where I was having a baby still felt so… Distant. So theoretical. But right then, I realized that what I was doing was bigger than myself. Bigger than the two of us. Definitely bigger than the acid in my stomach, the anger and the lingering desire.

"I came because I have to tell you something. I'm pregnant, Hades. I'm having your baby."

He stood there. Immobilized. He said nothing. For one long minute, he said nothing. And then, he looked at me. With a black fire that chilled me to my soul.

"This changes everything."

# CHAPTER SIX

I DIDN'T KNOW what to expect. He reached out and took me by the arm and began to propel me out of the grotto.

"You're certain?" he asked, just before we entered the church again.

"Of course I'm certain," I said. "I'm not the one that had a secret fiancée while we were… Yes, I'm certain."

"You are certain you're *pregnant*."

His eyes burned into mine. I could sense that he was at the end of his control. I'd experienced this in other ways, other places. When his desire for me had been beyond him. This was different.

"Yes. I took a test on the plane."

"And you're certain it's mine."

"It couldn't be anyone else's."

Ever. Because he was the only one. But I couldn't bring myself to say that, not now. Not while this was happening.

I was in shock, so I really didn't anticipate what he might do next. But he took me straight back to that room I had gone to only moments earlier and said that I was a florist. He knocked on the door, and it opened.

The maid of honor appeared again. "Hades," she said. "You can't see Jessica before the wedding."

"I will see my fiancée when I wish to. We have an important matter to discuss."

The maid of honor looked at me. "A flower matter?"

"Yes," he said.

He pushed his way into the room, bringing me with him, and looked around at all the bridesmaids. "Leave us," he said.

Jessica Lane was sitting there in front of the mirror, her dark hair styled into an artful updo.

I looked at her, and my stomach just about hit the floor. She was beautiful. In an iconic way. Soft and luxurious. Her dress was a cascade of silk, so beautiful and perfectly fitted to her. I was ruining her wedding day. Of course, I hadn't meant to. But that was the end result.

I felt so small then.

She saw me, and she frowned. "You're Florence Clare," she said.

"Yes," said Hades.

"What is this about?" Jessica asked.

"Things have changed," said Hades. "I'm sorry that this is happening right now. I will give you the allotted sum that we outlined in the prenuptial agreement."

"What?" she asked.

"We cannot get married."

Her jaw dropped. "Are you kidding me? We spent so much money."

"It was nothing to me," he said. "As is the money I offer you to go quietly."

"Hades," I said. "Are you for real right now? You were engaged to be married to her. You are practically jilting her at the altar. And you're offering her money? When you told me that your marriage wasn't going to change anything, I knew you were a cold-hearted bastard, but I had no idea…"

I didn't know why I was defending her. Or why it made me so angry. Maybe because in part I looked at her and saw a woman I had something in common with. I had been foolish enough to get into bed with him.

As had she, apparently. It was apparent now that led nowhere good.

"And what do you have to do with this?" she asked.

"She's having my baby," said Hades.

"Oh," said Jessica.

"I see you understand why this changes things," he said.

Jessica blinked. "Not really. Can't you just… Come up with an arrangement?"

"The arrangement is that she will be my wife. My child will not be a bastard."

"Unless he takes after his father," I said. And then I realized what *he* had just said. "Wait a minute. You think I'm going to marry you?"

"I know that you're going to marry me, *agape*. There is no question."

"Wait a minute," said Jessica. "You two hate each other. It's literally all over the news. I mean, there's some fanfic but, that's all."

I blinked. "There's what?"

"You know, it's when people write…"

"*I know what it is,*" I said. "Why is there…? That. About us?"

"Because some people think that your apparent hatred of each other is just disguising your desire to sleep together. And… It seems like it's true."

I couldn't understand what was happening. Because she should be crying. Throwing things. Maybe even threatening me. Instead, she was talking about the media.

"I'm really sorry," I said. "I didn't know about you. Not before… Not before the last time. There was one time when I did know, but I was really angry, and…"

"I'm not in love with him," she said. "He was looking for a dynastic bride, somebody who wanted to have his babies and take pictures in his gorgeous house. I have a media empire. It seemed like a good move. But I don't have any desire to get between you two. I mean, if we could have done a cool blended family thing for the internet, that would've been fine. But… I just need a way to come out of this looking good."

"You're a storyteller," he said. "Come up with something you have been doing ever since the engagement was announced. If you must make yourself into a victim, then do it, but don't paint Florence as a villain."

"No. People like to see women supporting other women these days. Also, you two are going to be a very big story." She tapped her chin. "Well. With all of my new money, I suppose I will embark on a year of wellness as I travel around the world. I'll do stirring posts about the importance of self-care. And how sometimes you have to get out of the way of true love."

*"Love!"* I sputtered. "I don't think he knows the meaning of the word."

Jessica laughed. "He doesn't. But then, neither do I. I'm a big can of self-love. But one reason that his proposition was so tempting was that it was going to leave me free to do whatever I wanted."

I felt like I was standing between two of the coldest people I had ever met. Jessica was likable, but I thought she had to be hollow inside. Because all she cared about was finding a way to spin the wedding. She didn't care that he was jilting her. In fact, it was almost like she thought being jilted was a bigger story, and therefore far more fun than wafting off to become a wife and mother.

"Perhaps you should escape the church dramatically in your gown. Maybe there is a photographer that can capture the image for you to put on your web page. You can claim that you had a feeling and had to follow your heart," he said.

"I like that. You really are very good with image."

I looked at him. And I was certain I was looking at a stranger. Yes. He was very good with image. But I wondered if there had ever been anything else there. Or if he had always been this…

This hollow man who saw people as playthings.

Perhaps I had deluded myself.

I had thrilled in his arrogance. I had let myself rage when he was stubborn. I had enjoyed the fight. Because in the end, I had believed there was something underneath that.

I had let myself believe that the man I let inside my body had more to him than that.

I had bought into a convenient lie, because I was no different than most women when it came to sex. I had told myself that we didn't have feelings for each other. But in the end, I'd had feelings.

Without another word, she slipped out of the room. I heard talking on the other side of the door. And I peered out for just one second, as she began to run down the stone corridor. And her maid of honor stood there, snapping photos on her phone.

I felt like I had just witnessed a play.

Because it was beginning to feel like a farce. That was for sure.

"Why didn't you tell me?" I asked. "That it was a marriage of convenience? Why were you even… Having one?"

"That's what you wish to talk about?"

I felt like I was sitting in the middle of the debris resulting from a detonated bomb. So picking which piece of detritus that we might talk about first seemed a little bit silly. It nearly didn't matter.

Because it was such a mess. How would we ever make sense of it?

He was supposed to be getting married in one hour.

"Is Sarah still here?"

"How did you know that Sarah was here?"

"I only assume that you would not come and do this without her. She is your best friend."

"She's here, but—"

"Excellent. I will have a selection of wedding gowns brought to you, what color bridesmaid dress would you prefer?"

"You are..." I sputtered. "*You are kidding me*. You think I'm going to marry you?"

"Yes," he said.

"I'm not marrying you. You were set to marry another woman not two minutes ago. I'm not going to be your backup just because I'm having a baby."

"I was marrying her to fulfill the terms of my father's will. I was to marry and produce children within a certain amount of time. I had five years. That has come to a close. You happen to already be pregnant with my child, and that is extremely convenient for me."

"Hades," I said. "You're forgetting something. We have kept this a secret for ten years because of the potential ramifications for our businesses. People are going to think that we... are price fixing and heading toward monopolizing areas of the marketplace. There might not just be financial consequences, there could be legal consequences."

"And we are going to have to work at figuring out how to manage that. We may have to dissolve different parts of the companies."

"Oh. Is this how you're going to get me to dissolve my space division."

"You don't have the NASA contract—you might as well."

Somehow, even in the middle of all of this, that enraged me. "And are you going to sell your cruise line to me?"

"Perhaps, Florence, but that is not my biggest concern at the moment."

My brain was spinning. His father had left a will saying he had to get married. He had to produce an heir. Technically, our child would be the heir to both companies. Unless we had more than one child.

I looked up at him. For one moment, it was like having an out-of-body experience. For one moment, I didn't understand why I shouldn't be wildly happy about this turn of events. Because he wasn't going to marry another woman. He was going to marry me.

He was on the phone.

He was ordering dresses.

"You didn't say what color," he said.

"Red," I said, and then clapped my hand over my mouth, because I was annoyed that I had answered the question at all. "My mother is in Italy," I said.

"Come now, Florence, don't you think that your mother will love the drama so much that she won't care that she couldn't be here? In fact, she'll probably like it better that she couldn't come, because it will allow her to tell the story and center herself as a victim of some kind."

I hated that he was right. And she wouldn't even really be mad at me because her new son-in-law would be a billionaire. And not only that, one that made for a sensational headline.

If nothing else, she would love it because my father would've hated it so much.

"I'm going to be sick," I said.

"Are you?"

For a moment, he looked genuinely concerned.

"I might be," I replied.

"We can stop for a moment, if you need."

"I haven't agreed to marry you."

"But you will," he said. "Because it makes the most sense."

"What happens to you if you don't marry?"

"The company reverts to the board."

"So you're telling me it would actually benefit me to not marry you."

"You're having my baby regardless. The production of an heir was the biggest issue. I am certain I could make the case to the lawyers that this counts. But is that honestly the legacy you want for the beginning of our child's life? Do you want to be your parents? Or worse, mine?"

We didn't talk about these things openly. I knew he didn't have a functional home life, even without knowing details. This was the first time it had occurred to me he might know the same about me.

I was still lost in the futility of everything. I had tried to hide myself from Hades, and apparently I wasn't as successful as I'd thought. I'd tried to hide us from the world, and now that was crumbling too.

My failures were mounting.

"But we kept it a secret," I said.

Mostly because the pain from the last ten years felt compounded in this moment. And futile. Because here we were. Ready to make this as public as we possibly could.

"If what Jessica says is true, we are poised to make a very popular move with the public. Many people will delight in being correct about the fact that we've been secretly carrying on for years."

I laughed. I couldn't help it. Maybe I was hysterical. It was entirely possible. "What was it all for? All of this. The years of sneaking around."

"Our fathers never knew. Your father never knew. I assume that's a big reason for the secrecy."

"If he knew that his grandchild was going to be…"

"We would both have lost our positions. There's no doubt about that."

Right then, all I wanted to do was let my guard down. All I wanted to do was to have another moment like the one we had in DC. When he'd come in and told me traffic had been terrible. When he kissed me. When he'd ordered me a cheeseburger because he knew exactly what I wanted.

That was what I craved. Another moment like that.

But I couldn't afford it.

I had to keep my wits about me.

"We have to get our legal team in here. Because there has to be a prenup."

"Wonderful. I'll put in another phone call. You keep all of your assets, I keep all of mine."

"Perfect," I said.

I knew him well enough to know if I defied him, he was going to start issuing threats. Still. I felt like it was time to give him the chance. To either be the man that I had wished he might be, or the man I knew him to be.

To tell me flat out he wouldn't be a monster. To say if I refused him he wouldn't try to destroy me professionally or personally.

I wanted to give him the chance to be…

Human.

"What if I walk away? What if I tell you you'll just have to deal with having your child on the weekends the way many men do."

The look on his face was enough to stop me cold. For the first time I realized that when he dealt with me he didn't unleash the full strength of his fury onto me. That he had never truly been the god of hell in my presence before.

The man I saw before me now, that man fit his name. Hades. That man would think nothing of dragging me down into the underworld along with him, where we could both burn together.

"I don't want to ruin you, Florence. But I will. We both know that a big reason you didn't want our affair coming out was the way you would be looked at as a woman sleeping with her competitor. If I let slip the wrong thing, imagine what it will do to your employees' confidence in you. To your investors' confidence. People might even be tempted to imagine I had the upper hand when it came to the NASA contracts because you took information from me and they realized it."

My stomach went cold. "I didn't."

"Later, I saw the proposal you put forward. Sections were alarmingly similar to mine."

"You know that I didn't take anything from you. We were very careful. I never wanted you to blame me for anything like that, and I know you wanted the same."

"It is not about what happened, it is about what is believable. And you know it."

"You would do that to me."

"I would. Where you got the idea that I am soft or movable, I don't know. But I learned one thing from my father of any value, and that is to never bend. I will have what is mine. The child is mine. You are mine."

"You," I said, "are not the man I hoped you were."

He didn't care about what I wanted. His priority would be what he saw as the right thing, whether I agreed or not. I was gutted to have it confirmed.

But I'd had to know. For sure. Because if I was going to do this, then I had to protect myself. If I was going to marry Hades, then I had to remember who he was, and who I was.

This was never going to be a union about feelings. Just like everything that had happened between us before this was not about feelings.

It was about control. It was about possession. Obsession. But it had never been about feelings.

"You will walk down that aisle toward me in forty-five minutes. Be ready."

# CHAPTER SEVEN

Sarah and an entire team came into the room. Her eyes were wide, and she was looking around as if she was checking to see if someone was holding a gun on me.

"Are you actually insane?"

A red dress was thrust toward her. "Thanks," she said. "You're not marrying him."

"I am," I said. Because I knew that I had no other choice.

Or maybe you don't want a different choice. Maybe you're a sad deluded girl who thinks that this is a fairy tale.

No. I didn't. I knew who he was.

I knew…

"Is he blackmailing you?"

"Sort of. But I wouldn't expect anything different from him."

"You don't have to do this."

"Believe me. The wreckage if I don't isn't worth it."

If the various hairstylists and makeup artists were interested in exactly what was going on, they certainly didn't show it. A stylist looked at me critically and then took three different gowns off a rack that she apparently had determined would be best for me.

One of them was made from layers of floating, diaphanous material, the bodice draped over my curves with soft pleats. The skirt swished with each movement. It was the kind of thing that spoke of femininity. On a level that I normally would never allow myself to project.

I looked like a bride.

Next to Hades in a severe black suit, I would look nothing less than *soft*. It was the kind of thing that I would never risk in a meeting. But at a wedding?

Our wedding.

I looked at myself in the mirror. My eyes were large, my skin waxen.

Did I look like the spoils? Would he appear to be the victor?

I looked beautiful and I didn't know how to feel about it. Just like I had no idea how to feel about becoming a mother. About becoming a wife.

The wife of hell, basically.

But the only hell I'd ever willingly flung myself into, so it wasn't like I didn't know how I'd gotten here.

Play with hellfire and you might get damned.

"This is the one," the woman said.

"Perhaps something more tailored," I said.

A bid to try and find my balance. My comfort. In the middle of something that could not be less comfortable.

"No," she said. "This one suits you."

I knew that it did. And I knew that I loved it. It was only that something about it was terrifying. Like going into battle naked when what I needed was armor. Only I didn't have time to protest. Because then I was draped in a towel and given hairstyling and makeup. Bright blush to cover up the insipid color of my skin. Pink lipstick.

My hair was styled down. Loose, flowing curls.

For all the world to see, it would look like I had surrendered my power to Hades.

This was how he won. I hadn't seen that when I'd left Lake Como. All I'd thought about was that it was a race against time, and I had to win it. I'd made the classic mistake of not looking far enough ahead.

I had thought that I needed to get here so that I could give Jessica the chance to make a choice.

In the end, he had managed to twist it and make it so I had little time to make a choice of my own.

I could make him wait. And maybe I should have, but instead I was standing there in a wedding dress. I'd let him take control of this situation because I was still too shell-shocked by the last twelve hours to be anything but.

Or maybe I'd allowed it because the teenage girl who'd once thought she loved Hades still lived somewhere inside me.

Hadn't I learned better over these last ten years? Ten years of fraught sex. And he'd never grown closer to me. His moods were what made us. His intensity driving our encounters. He thought he set the rules, and I'd let him.

That was why he'd said nothing had to change, even after his engagement. Because he thought he got to decide. And what I wanted didn't matter.

Because I was nothing to him. Nothing but an outlet for his darkest, basest needs. Because there was no need to get me to sign an NDA, after all.

Who would I tell?

He knew, of any lover he could have possibly had, I would be the one most motivated to keep all of his secrets in order to preserve my own self.

Before I knew it, the hour had passed and I was being ushered out of the dressing room. A dressing room that one hour ago had contained a bridal party and a whole different bride. Would the sanctuary be empty? What had he told the guests? Would I be marrying him in front of Jessica's friends and family?

I stood outside the sanctuary wringing my hands, and Sarah was directed inside. She looked at me, as if waiting to be told the whole thing would be called off. But I didn't call it off. So, in she went.

I felt another presence in the antechamber and turned.

My half brother Javier was standing there, looking severe. We hadn't grown up together, but over the years he, Rocco and I had found some sort of rapport. I was shocked to see him here. "How did you…"

"I know Hades. He called because he knew I was in the city."

My half brother was friends with my nemesis. I'd had a feeling they might be. I wasn't shocked neither of them had ever mentioned it.

*Nemesis? You're marrying him.*

*True.*

"Oh." He'd come to my wedding. Last minute. I was so weirdly touched by it.

"Rocco sends his regrets that he couldn't make it. He's in Italy, so of course there was no way for him to fly in on time."

I laughed, though I didn't find any of this all that amusing. "Well, it was my fault for replacing the bride at the last minute."

"Do you need help?" he asked.

Did I? I wasn't sure. I was tempted to take it. Tempted to ask him to get us a helicopter and get us the heck out of Dodge.

I shook my head. "No, Javier. I don't. These are the consequences of my actions."

My brother treated me to one raised brow. "I hope that's in your wedding vows."

"What do you think marriage is?" I asked.

It was more a genuine question than I had meant it to be.

"If you ask our mother, a moneymaking venture." He stared ahead for a moment. "I'm not sure I can answer that. Or, not sure I should."

"Tell me."

"I don't believe in love, *hermanita.* At least not in the way of fairy tales. I believe in loyalty, and I believe in family. There is love in that. Otherwise I think it is a way we try and make lust into something palatable. A way for men to keep women with them so they can be certain their offspring are theirs."

"Romantic," I said, dryly, thinking about my and Hades' *offspring* then.

"Why are you marrying him?"

I looked up at the ceiling. "Offspring."

"Ah. Congratulations."

I gave him a disparaging look. "You don't mean that."

He looked back at me, the glint in his eye familiar to me. I'd seen it in the mirror enough times. Strange. I'd always associated that steel with my father, but Javier and I shared a mother.

It made me wonder how much steel I missed in our mother because she camouflaged it so well with all the softness I'd always thought would make a woman seem weak.

"I do," he said. "A person needs heirs to carry on a legacy."

What was my legacy actually going to be? I'd never been less certain.

The doors to the sanctuary swung open, and my brother extended his arm. "Come, let me walk you down the aisle."

"Are you giving me away, Javier?"

"Only you can give yourself away. I'm simply there to provide backup if you decide you need to run."

The music changed and we began to walk forward.

*Run.*

The word echoed inside of me. As we made our way down the long aisle. And then I looked up, and I saw him. Standing there looking severe. Looking every inch the ruthless monster who had made threats to me in the form of a marriage proposal.

Looking every inch the avenging angel he so often was when he appeared in my hotel rooms, ready to claim me, take me.

Looking like the man I sparred with in boardrooms.

The man I surrendered to in bedrooms.

Hades was far too many things to me to ever be simple. And running would never solve the problem.

It hadn't yet.

Now he was going to be the father of my child. That was something I could barely wrap my head around. Because it required me fully taking on board the fact that I was going to be a mother.

I knew how to parent in the way my father had. I could imagine it. After all, I was also dedicated to my work. Dedicated to Edison. Dedicated to the future, to the family legacy.

But there was something missing from that. And I knew it. I also would never be my mother. Didn't want to be. Suddenly, I felt like I was falling through a void. Toward a man who knew as little about being a father as I knew about being a mother. What were we doing?

Would the child be raised by nannies? While he and I continued to battle against each other?

I couldn't see it. I couldn't even understand it.

But far too soon, we had arrived at the head of the aisle, and Hades reached his hand out to me.

I already knew there was no other option but to take it. I already knew that the devil's bargain had been made. Perhaps sealed with a kiss ten years ago, on my eighteenth birthday.

Perhaps then I had sealed my own fate.

Perhaps there had never been a different outcome.

Eventually, we were bound to be careless. In one way or another. Whether it was pregnancy, being discovered by the press or something else entirely, we had been destined for destruction. I had to figure out a way to make sure we didn't destroy the baby we had created.

I had to.

I was smart, and I could figure it out. I could figure out how to do this.

Maybe I would bring the baby with me to work.

I was going to be exposed as being a female. I was going to be a pregnant CEO. One who had fallen in the basest way. One who had slept with her business rival. And then married him.

There was no more hope left for me to wander through this landscape an untouchable robot.

There was a freedom in this disaster I had not anticipated.

I had made a mistake.

The biggest mistake, and it was being broadcast to the world even now.

His wedding had been upended. I was going to be portrayed as a home-wrecker, at least in part, whether Jessica was able to control the narrative or not.

Some people would enjoy the spectacle of us being together. Others would scoff.

And I had no control.

For the first time in my life, I felt the freedom in the surrender of that.

His dark eyes caught mine, and my stomach went hollow.

No. It wasn't for the first time.

Because I had found freedom in surrender and Hades' arms before. That had always been a part of who I was. But I had never understood how I could live my life that way.

I suddenly did.

I might not have all the logistics together, but I was not devastated.

I had lost control. And that meant no more trying so hard to hold it all together. No more desperate attempts at making sure the narrative was in my power. It wasn't. Nothing was.

I took Hades' hand, and he brought me to the head of the altar, facing him.

I looked out at the audience and tried to see who I recognized there.

It was full of Jessica's friends and family. Because everyone was glued to the spectacle.

And so I would give them one. Because the only acceptable way to spin this was…

I had to be the opposite of everything I had been up until now. I had to be soft. I had to be absolutely overcome by emotion. I was. It wasn't hard for me to play that part. I was angry, yes, frightened. But I was also…

Enthralled with him. As I had ever been.

The feelings that I had for Hades were complicated. I had wanted to call it *hate*, but it had never been able to be contained in such a short, simple word. Not honestly.

It was now, and had ever been, something bigger than the both of us. And so now, I did my best to let that show.

One thing that was never in short supply between us was passion. So I looked at him, with every ounce of passion that I had ever felt for him. And I felt a ripple move through the room.

Because our chemistry was undeniable. That much I knew.

What I hoped, was that this moment would seem undeniable to the people around us. As inevitable and essential as it suddenly did to me.

I could see a dark flame in his eyes. He felt it.

Good.

In some ways, I wanted to punish him. Here in front of everybody. He had been prepared to give himself to another woman. To make vows to another woman. On some level, I had been contending with my feelings of being the woman scorned for weeks now, and it felt good to remind him of what he had nearly lost.

The priest began to recite an extremely benign wedding script. It might have been for Jessica and Hades. It might have been for Hades and me. It didn't make a difference.

And I wouldn't allow it to be a problem.

Because I had found a small scrap of control within myself, and I would not surrender it. Not for anything. I would not allow him to see me crack.

So I made vows to him, promised myself to him, publicly, made vows that I had been keeping for the past ten years. Forsaking all others. Clinging only to him.

I had done all these things. Even as I had told him, told myself, that he was my nemesis.

He had nearly married another woman.

That stabbed me.

It wasn't fair, perhaps. Because I had never intended to take this public. Not ever. I had, somewhere in the back of my mind, imagined that I might marry someone else someday.

Still, he had devastated me.

But now I was here. I was the one having his baby.

I was the one marrying him.

It was time for us to kiss then.

I knew a moment of very real fear. What would it be like to kiss him in full view of all these people? What would it be like to kiss him and have to stop?

That had never happened. Because we kissed in private, behind locked doors. We kissed when we knew that the kiss was tinder for a fire we would let rage all night long.

We did not kiss as a destination.

And we certainly didn't do it with an audience.

He wrapped his arm around my waist then, his other hand going to grip my chin. My breath left my body. When he touched me like this, it was always the end for me. The end of my control. The end of everything.

There was nothing but this. Nothing but those

dark eyes burning into mine. That dominant hold, the promise of what would come later.

We didn't have to manufacture a kiss for the crowd. We had to find a way to keep from revealing ourselves entirely.

The kiss was carnal. It was all we knew. I kissed him back, because I was now, as ever, powerless to do anything but surrender to the driving need between us. In truth, if we could control it we would have. If we could have found control now, it would have made a mockery of all that had occurred before. It would have indicated we might have been able to stop this. But I already knew we couldn't have.

It was, in that sense, a relief to be lost.

A relief to prove we had no other choice. Then and now.

When we parted, he was breathing as hard as I was. I knew it hadn't been a show. The wounded lover inside of me wanted to claim that as a trophy. And I let her.

I was surprised when Hades addressed the crowd.

"My wife and I will not be staying for the reception, but I invite all of you to do so. Enjoy the cake. Enjoy the party. We have some things to discuss."

And with that, he gripped my hand and began to walk me down the aisle. I heard very fast footsteps behind us, and I turned to see Sarah close.

My brother was not far behind.

The four of us arrived in the antechamber of the sanctuary.

"You don't have to go with him," said Sarah.

Javier looked at her. "No," he said. "She doesn't."

"I'm going with him," I said. "Thank you. For being here with me."

Hades regarded both Sarah and Javier. "Your protective natures are admirable. But Florence made her choice when she came here today. She knows that."

I did. It was clear then, when he said that. I had always known what would happen. Somewhere, deep down. I had known he would marry Jessica. Not if I was carrying his baby.

I had known that he would feel a need to make his child legitimate. Because that was who Hades was. He was a businessman, in all things, and that meant acquisition was the purest of things in his mind.

He had acquired me.

He had acquired a baby.

In one fell swoop.

*But that means that you've also acquired him.*

It went both ways. It always had between us. I was not, nor had I ever been helpless. I had never been a damsel in distress. I had gone to him the first time. I was the one who had made it clear that I wanted to take the simmering attraction between us and turn it into something real.

I had more power here than even I had realized when I had first decided to go to the church.

Yes. I had much more power here than I had given myself credit for.

"I'm all right," I said.

"You're much more than all right," Hades said, propelling me out of the church and down the stairs, toward the limousine that had just pulled up to the curb. That was when I realized paparazzi were everywhere. Flashbulbs went off all around us. And he wrapped his arm around my waist, holding me up against him, pressing one hand to the top of the limousine, my body wedged against the open door. "You've won," he said.

And then he claimed my mouth. And I was lost.

# CHAPTER EIGHT

We didn't speak to each other in the car. I was entirely too frayed around the edges to form an intelligent sentence, so I didn't bother.

Instead, I stared out the window, up at the towering buildings.

"No questions, *agape*?"

*You've won.*

What had I won? I had just been forced down the aisle and now I was following him wherever it was he had decided to take me.

"What did you mean I won?"

He looked at me, and for a moment I saw a crack. "You didn't want me to marry her," he said.

Rage spiked in my blood. "No, Hades. I don't care what you do or who you marry. What I care about is that you didn't tell me. What I care about is that you thought I was the type of woman who wouldn't care that you'd married someone else. What I care about is that I treated you like an equal, a rival. You treated me like a whore."

He growled, the feral sound shocking me. "I did not treat you that way. You assume I could stop this,

Florence. And that is what you don't understand. You have won because in the end my well-ordered plans are for nothing. Because of you."

His words left my stomach churning, rage rolling through me. Unease.

I wasn't surprised when we ended up at the airport.

I just needed a moment. To simply move. To react. Not fight against him, not try to plan the next move. But to breathe.

It wasn't until we were on the plane—a plane we had made love on before—that I decided it was time to figure out what the plan was.

"Where are we going?"

"We have at least six hours until we land in Switzerland."

"Hoping the famously neutral country will help in our communication?"

"No. I have a chalet there. Perfectly out-of-the-way and impossible to access if one does not have a helicopter. Well stocked. It will see us through this initial storm, and the holidays. Isn't that romantic. Off on a secluded Christmas honeymoon."

It made my stomach churn. Because I had been thinking about how lovely it was that he and I would have a month together in New York, just a while ago. It hadn't gone that way.

And now we would be shut in a house together. Albeit, a house that I assumed was large enough we could also never run into each other if we wanted. It didn't fill me with the same sort of uncomplicated thrill that it had two months ago.

Though it did still thrill me. Even if it was a dark, twisted sort of feeling.

"We have six hours," he repeated. "Plenty of time to cover whatever ground you need."

"I haven't slept." And I didn't think that I could sleep even if I wanted to. Not after all of that. I was utterly and completely undone by the events of the day, but it had left me supercharged.

"Sleep if you wish," he said.

I wouldn't let him tell me what to do on top of everything else, even though I was so tired I was in danger of losing consciousness in my seat. "I don't. What is the plan? Do you honestly expect us to be married forever?"

"I don't see why not. This makes sense. We can make it work. Why be competitors? What would be the end result of our continuing on the way we have been anyway? We would destroy one another eventually, I assume. I don't actually want to destroy you, Florence."

I looked at him, my stomach sour. "Then what is it you want?"

He lifted a dark brow. "I want to navigate this without our empires crumbling. It would be best if you were a help and not a hindrance."

"Hades, I am carrying your baby. I never had to tell you. I chose to come and speak to you. I chose to handle this with as much integrity as I could. I chose to keep the pregnancy. I chose to walk down that aisle toward you. I had ample opportunity to escape. Do you not think my brother was standing by with the means to spirit me out of the city if I wanted him to? I chose to marry you. You might ask yourself why."

"Because I threatened you."

"Because it is useful to me. You underestimate me. At every turn. I have the control here. I could have denied you access to this child, and you know it. The whole world was ignorant to the fact that we were together. I could have let you marry her. I could have let you have your children with her."

"But you couldn't," he said, his eyes dark, burning into mine. "Or you would have. You wouldn't let her have me."

"You bastard. You let me find out about your engagement in the press. You were as cruel as you could have been, and that was a choice. You…" I stood up. "Let's talk about it then, Hades. Let's talk about the ways in which you are *the actual devil*."

"You and I had a sexual relationship," he said. His gaze was dispassionate then. A stranger's. "I never promised you fidelity of any kind. Likewise, I never promised Jessica fidelity. When I told you my engagement changed nothing, I was being honest with you."

"But you didn't explain it to me."

"Given the nature of our relationship I didn't think it mattered."

That made me even angrier. "You treated it like a business matter. You were the CEO of the sex so it didn't matter what I thought because I'm just beneath you. Because you never saw me as a human being, did you?"

He looked past me. "As you said yourself. I'm the

very god of hell. And think about that, Florence. That is what my father chose to name me. Whether that speaks to his view on me, or what he hoped I would become, is nearly irrelevant. I was never shaped in the mold of a good man. And I never pretended to be. You… You came to me. Far too innocent, and far too young. I should've turned you away."

"But you didn't. Not once. Not once over the last decade," I said.

"Guilty." His dark eyes gleamed. "And you kept coming back."

That was the truth. The ugly, awful truth of it. There was no innocent party here. We'd used each other. He'd never gotten to know me, but I'd never gotten to know him either. I'd put the company, my reputation above any potential relationship with him.

I had thought I might be as cold as he was at one time.

I didn't feel cold now.

I felt raw. Bruised.

"This is our consequence, I suppose," I said, quietly.

He reached over and poured himself a glass of whiskey, settled deep into the couch and stared across the expanse of space between us. "Quite the consequence. You might as well vent your rage at me. Get it over with."

He said it so casually. So dry. So…controlled. As if none of this touched him. As if he could be here with me or with Jessica and it would make no difference to him. As if my feelings were an inconvenience he would allow just for the moment.

"Is that what you think this is? That I'm… Angry and need to vent?" It wasn't untrue. But there was so much more to it. Of course, I hadn't even begun to work out what all my feelings were, so I felt like I was treading on dangerous ground.

"It seems as if that's the case."

"What did you feel?" I was so angry at him. He was such an impenetrable wall. I knew him in business. And I knew him in bed. And in the time in between he had gotten so much more of me. Because I had shown my hand, hadn't I? I had shown my hurt over his engagement. I had gone to him and given him that loss of control. Even if I had scraped some power back by reminding him that I'd chosen to tell him about the baby, I was the one who'd given more of my…heart. And what had he given me?

Nothing.

An orgasm.

A child.

Our consequence.

And yet I was no closer to having any idea of what he felt for anyone or anything. Perhaps he really did feel nothing. I'd known a moment of true relief followed by true panic listening to him and Jessica worked out the story for the dissolution of their engagement. Because both of them had been so utterly dispassionate. So cold. As if they were made of stone.

Meanwhile I was not made of anything of the kind. I knew that now.

I was entirely made of the sorts of feelings I didn't want at all.

"When?"

"When I denied you. When I told you that I wouldn't be with you anymore after you were married. Did you feel anything?"

He leaned back, a shadow concealing part of his face. He was starkly beautiful. High cheekbones, a square jaw, that mouth that had done so many wicked things to me. I could barely catch my breath when I looked at him.

"I knew you would never be able to manage it." He took a sip of his whiskey, all arrogance. "If you had been able to control yourself with me, *agape*, you would have done so years ago."

"You're wrong." At least I was confident that I was telling the truth. "I wouldn't have shared you. Do you have any idea how angry I was, knowing that you had slept with me while you were planning to marry somebody else?"

"It angered you that I was having sex with another woman during our time together?"

"Of course it did. But I never thought that I had an exclusive claim to your body, Hades. I did not think that you would get engaged without at least speaking to me."

He frowned. "So it is the perceived emotional betrayal that bothers you? Even though you and I have never had anything like a relationship?"

"Yes."

It all bothered me. In truth.

"Put your mind at ease, Florence. I did not love her. Neither was I sleeping with her."

I let that truth settle over me. I had figured at that point that he didn't love her, but the idea that he hadn't slept with the woman—who had been exceedingly beautiful—had not occurred to me.

"Why didn't you tell me that?"

Yet again, it was like the mask slipped. Giving me a view of something more feral. An intensity normally reserved for sex.

"Because. Because it would've been better if you would've stayed away. Don't you think? It would have been better if I could have married her and kept you away from me." It was an intensity that I was only used to when we were engaged in work battles and bedroom games. It was not something I was used to in conversation with him. But then, we didn't do conversation. We didn't talk. We didn't share pieces of ourselves. Only our bodies.

"If you think that, then why did you marry me at all? Why did you… In your office that day, why have me then. If you were getting married to get rid of me, then why? Because if you hadn't, and if you would have remembered the condom, we wouldn't be in this situation."

He was across the space, and over to me before I could draw my next breath. His large hand resting against the base of my throat. "Because if I could, I would have. As it is for you, it is for me. You know that."

The words were like a balm to all those wounds in

my spirit. It was easy to believe that it wasn't as enthralling for him as it was for me. Easy to believe he had other lovers, that this was just one flavor of sex he enjoyed.

But his face now told me otherwise.

I really was his shame.

If he wasn't a slave to it, the same as I was, he would never touch me.

But he had touched me. Over and over again for years.

I had power here. I needed to remember that.

"I do," I said. "So why sit there and hurl those things at me like accusations, when you know you are no better."

His lips curved, his body relaxed and he moved back to the couch across from me. My heart was pounding hard. Not with fear.

With desire.

Because it was always like this. It didn't matter if it should be. It didn't matter if it was wrong, toxic, obsessive.

It was always this.

If we could have stopped, we would have stopped.

"I act with control at all times, Florence." He took another sip of his scotch. "I understand that you may not know that. Because the one exception to that in all of my life has been you. I knew that I shouldn't touch you. That first time you came to me, I knew. Do you have any idea… If my father had found out, let's just say the punishment likely would not have been worth the reward I found in your arms. And yet. I made the same mistake with you. Over and over again. I let myself have you, even knowing that I should not. When I saw the terms of my father's will, I saw a means of escaping it. When the time ran out, I knew that I had to choose a wife, and when I found Jessica, I knew that I had found someone with goals that were the same as my own. She did not want love. She needed to marry to help inject something new into her image. I needed to fulfill the terms of the will. Both of us needed to fulfill external obligations."

I watched him, the way that he moved, the way that he spoke. I was fascinated by him. Because this was not the kind of thing we ever engaged in. This was more conversation than we ever had.

I felt desperate then. To close this gap between us. And yet, I knew that it would be foolish. Dangerous. Already…

I had said that he felt the same way I did, but I feared it wasn't true.

Already, I feared that my feelings ran far deeper than his.

I refused, utterly refused, to name them.

Anyway, if I thought that I felt something… Anything like love for him, I was simply delusional. A woman looking to explain away her behavior as something other than pure unadulterated lust. We didn't know each other. And what I did know about him did not make him the sort of man I ought to have feelings for.

Sex wasn't love.

I knew that.

Respect in business was not love.

But right then, my mind clicked back to the first thing he had said.

"What do you mean your father would've punished you?"

"I mean exactly that. My father ran his company with an iron fist. And he ran his home the same way. My mother was not like your mother, Florence. She did not run away seeking adventure. She sought safety. Peace. But had she taken my father's heir with her, my father would've never stopped looking for her. She had to find safety, and to do that she had to leave me. Without his preferred target for his rages, my father had to adjust his focus on to me."

I didn't know what to say to that. Because of all the things that I had thought about his father, and the relationship Hades might've had with him, I hadn't ever considered that he was physically abusive.

There were no rumors about it in the media. Nothing.

He was such a strong man, and proud. Hard. Things that made him impenetrable at times, but the idea of him being…harmed by his own father. Broken. I hated that. Whatever anger I felt for him was replaced by shock. By the unending sadness that I felt thinking about how he'd been hurt…and I hadn't known.

His father's death had been a shock. He'd been healthy, and while her own father hadn't liked him at all, he'd been strangely upset about the death of his rival. Or perhaps it was death in general. He'd died two years later of a heart attack. I supposed there was a lesson there about overworking yourself.

I didn't know how to learn it.

"Hades…"

"It is nothing. Do not waste your tears for me, a child who grew up with access to the greatest education, the best means of travel in the world. There are many in life who have struggles, and I would not consider myself one of them."

"Your father physically abused you, and you don't consider that a struggle," I asked, feeling incredulous.

"No. If I did, perhaps I would speak of it with a therapist. As it stands, I'm fine."

I looked at the strong, remote man sitting across from me, and I had to ask myself how he thought he was fine. How I had ever thought he was fine.

What I knew about him for certain was that he was a wall. Until the wall came down, and then he was passion personified. And then he was fire.

*Are you any different?*

Maybe not. Maybe I compartmentalized things just the same as he did.

Maybe I had to keep myself protected too. But it didn't come from a place of having been… Abused.

"I'm sorry," I said. "I wish I would have known. All that time we knew each other… You were twenty-one the first time we were together."

"If my father had access to me, then he would hit me. And I allowed it, because… He told me that if I ever displeased him, he would find my mother. And he would kill her. I had no reason to disbelieve him."

"Why are you only now telling me this?"

"Because we have only now just decided to have a conversation. You are marrying me, and you need to know the manner of man you've married. My father wasn't a safe man. I never had any desire for a passionate marriage. Things… They will not be the same between us now."

I tried to process that. Tried to understand what he was saying. "You think that we are suddenly going to not have passion between us?"

"We have to figure out how to arrange our lives so that we can work together. Things have changed. Where once we could fight one another, act as opponents, we cannot now. We are having a child."

"I understand that."

"I don't know how to be a good father," he said.

It felt like a warning. Combined with what he'd just shared with me about his father but… I was angry with Hades. Hurt. But I wasn't hurt enough to allow myself to believe he was the sort of monster his father had been.

Yes, he'd hurt me.

He would never hurt me physically.

I had been with him for ten years. Even if it wasn't a relationship. He had been my lover.

He was difficult. He wasn't evil.

"I don't know how to be a good mother. And I realized as I walked toward you down that aisle that we are both ill-suited to this, but it is what's happened. We will make it work."

"We must make it work," he said. "Sometimes I

think my father simply wanted me to have a child because what he really wanted was for me to pass down the pain he meted out on to me. He said that once. That when I had children I would understand. What a trial they are. How difficult it is to try and shape one in the way that you need them shaped. He said one day I would understand."

"Your father was weak," I said. I had many opinions about his father, mostly given to me by my own father, but none of them had been about his actions as a man. They had simply been about the way he ran his business. My father had known. But I knew now. "A weak man has to rule with tyranny. That isn't you. It never has been. You might not have always been my favorite person, Hades, but I have always respected you. I have always respected the brilliance that you brought into our competitiveness. I have always preferred going up against you than anyone that I could beat easily. And you have enjoyed the fight as well. The truth is, you've never tried to crush me. Not even once. Because that doesn't bring you joy. You like a fight. But you're not a bully. They are two different things."

"I will never touch our child in anger," he said. "You have my vow."

I believed him. Because hadn't he experienced enough uncertainty? A mother who had left him for her own safety. A father who had used his fists on him.

I felt despairing.

For him. The child he'd been. The man that he was.

The man I had known all this time, who perhaps could've at least been my friend, whose pain I might have known, and yet I didn't, because I had been so focused on him as an object of desire.

And then later as my competition.

"We will merge the companies. There is no other option. We simply will not be able to conduct them as two separate entities. Nobody would believe it was possible, first of all."

"I don't like that," I said.

"Think about it," he said. "The heir to your throne is now the heir to mine. And so what difference does it make if we keep them separate for the next thirty years? Eventually, the company will belong to our child. And so, we might as well make them into one."

I couldn't deny that he had a point. I also felt like he was doing his level best to try and push the conversation away from personal things.

"What about fidelity?" I asked.

"That has nothing to do with our companies."

"It is the holiday season and we have gone away for a honeymoon. I say we wait to speak about the logistics of the companies."

"Not something I would have expected to hear from you."

"Well, I didn't expect to be married and having a child either. I find the topic more concerning than I did only twenty-four hours ago."

"The truth is, we have to come to a consensus on what we're going to do with the company and release a joint statement by tomorrow."

"Why?"

"Because it matters," he said. "Because we cannot afford to have any speculation or accusation that we do not have total control over what's happening. Do you not understand that? I have taken a contract with the government, and nothing can appear untoward."

There was a level of intensity to him that I had experienced in business meetings, but there was something different as well. I wondered if it had to do with what he just told me about his father.

There had been punishments. When he had made mistakes, he had been hurt.

That was what he was acting like now. As if a mistake was going to come with a heavy price.

"Then we can merge," I said.

I felt myself give. But it did not feel weak. I didn't feel like I was letting him win. I felt like I was finding a path to peace in my own life. Like I was taking this moment and turning it into something better. I'd had the epiphany standing there at the altar that there was something powerful in this loss of control. I experienced it again just now.

I had always imagined that my spine was a core of steel. Because when it came to dealing with my parents, I felt like I had to bend too often. But this was not a reshaping of myself. It was a strength. He was being rigid, and he couldn't find his way around it.

But I could.

"I will—"

"We must maintain equal power in the company," I said.

He looked at me. "My company is worth more."

"I don't care."

"That simply isn't how these things work."

On this, I would not bend. "I've worked far too hard to surrender everything to you now."

"Perhaps you should've thought of that before you surrendered to me the way you did in my office."

"Which of us surrendered truly, Hades? Can you answer that question?"

His lip curled. "We will have equal positions," he said.

"Good. Come now, you would not wish to elevate yourself above me using blackmail. I don't even believe you would ruin me if you had the chance. Because again, you're not a bully. You don't want uncontested power. You want a fight, because it makes you better, and you know it. We have always made each other better. Iron sharpening iron."

He chuckled. "Perhaps. Though in my experience when a person with a hard head goes up against another it is usually bone bruising flesh."

I let the silence lapse between us, and I tried to imagine the treatment he had received from his father. Let it reshape the things I'd assumed about him all that time ago.

I had thought that he had been his father's pride.

I would never have assumed that Hades was being physically harmed by his father.

Not ever.

"You can tell me," I said.

"Do you really want to hear this? I will say the

worst of it is always what ends up in the mind. With the body…you can learn to shut yourself down. But when you are locked away for days at a time. When your father buys you things only to destroy them…" His throat worked. "That was the only reason he ever gave me anything. To make me care for it, so that it could be used against me." His smile then was like a dagger. "He loved Christmas. He would make an elaborate setup and throw a huge party for his clients. He would wrap presents and put them beneath the tree. Sometimes none would be for me. Other times there would be. One year he burned them all, wrapped, in the yard." He frowned. "The worst, I think, was never getting to know what they were."

"That's horrible. Despicable. You don't have to have had a good father to know that's wrong and you would never do it."

He shook his head. "No. I never would."

Silence between us was dangerous, because the minute we stopped speaking, there was only tension to fill the space between us.

"The matter of our marriage," I said.

"Yes?"

"I don't want to share you."

He looked at me, as though he pitied me. "You will regret that, later. When you are tired of our fighting. When you are weary of having to deal with my moods."

I didn't understand why he couldn't simply tell me what he wanted rather than speaking in riddles. But then I supposed this highlighted the true problem. I had known him for all of these years and never really known him.

"What is it you wanted from a wife?"

"I told you. Children, and no demand on me. I did not wish to get married to make my life more complicated. I wanted to get married to solve a problem. That's all."

I felt like my chest had been punctured. "And I've never been much of a solution, have I?"

"No," he bit out. "If you think this is a convenience to me, you would be incorrect."

I still felt…sorry for him. But that gave him no excuse for trying to hurt me. Simply because he was trying to force distance back between us.

"I'm tired," I said. "I'm going to bed." I stood up. "I already know where the bedroom is."

And then I left him there, and some part of myself.

Things were already too complicated without splintering my feelings for him even more.

I was angry at him. For being…

Human.

I preferred him to be the devil.

Because at least then I could fight against him with no pity whatsoever.

# CHAPTER NINE

I WOKE AS we touched down in Switzerland. I felt disoriented for a moment. And then the nausea reminded me. I was pregnant. And I had married Hades.

I had little time to marinate on that before the bedroom door opened. I had changed into a luxurious sweat suit I'd found hanging in the closet before going to sleep—I chose not to ponder whether it was for Jessica or for me.

"Are you well?" he asked.

"Not especially," I said.

But it didn't matter, because we were landing. I changed into a dress I found in the closet and soon we were transferred from the airplane to a helicopter. And I couldn't help myself, I clung to his arm as the unwieldy vehicle took off in the wind.

He put his hand over mine, a gesture so comforting it made my eyes well up with tears, and it made me want to punch myself. Because I shouldn't go getting emotional over him. Not when he didn't actually care about me. Physical connection was something we had. But we'd never had anything more.

It took twenty minutes in the helicopter for us to arrive at the top of a snowy peak, surrounded by white-capped pine trees, and an awe-inspiring vista of the Alps. It was definitely a place to go to disappear.

We got out of the helicopter, and the chill from the wind shocked me. He shielded me with his body as we walked toward the house. He put his fingerprints up against a pad on the door, and it unlocked, allowing us entry.

The interior was stunning. All light pine and glass that looked out over the craggy Alps. We were cocooned in silence, wrapped in the blanket of all that snow.

For the first time in my life, I was alone with him and it wasn't only for a matter of hours. For the first time, we weren't a secret. The whole world knew about us.

But here it didn't feel like the world existed.

Bizarrely, I found myself thankful he'd taken us here. Bizarre because I didn't think I really owed him thanks for much of anything right now.

He pushed a button on the wall and the glass-encased fireplace roared to life. I could see through it, straight to the outside, where the flames danced on the snow. There was a time when I would have relished this. A chance to spend days exploring his body? A chance to try and exhaust some of the need that constantly burned between us?

But it was different now. This wasn't temporary.

We were looking at something much more permanent.

I had never dreamed of forever with Hades. Though

in some ways I'd dreaded it. The idea that I would never be able to want any other man. That I would end up alone because my body had found his, so my heart would never find anyone.

This was the inglorious inevitable.

Here we were, expecting a child. Married. And yet we were the same two people who met in secret rooms and communicated using only our bodies. We had no practice at this.

We were competitors. We had never shared our personal space.

Though, looking around this room, I could not say whether or not there was anything especially personal about it.

"How long have you had this house?"

"Five years or so," he said, discarding his suit jacket, mesmerizing me as he undid the cuffs on his white shirt and began to roll the sleeves up over his forearms.

In the past, that would have been an invitation to only one thing. I could imagine what might have happened only a few months ago with ease. Everything about his body had always excited me.

I really did like his forearms.

I tried to focus on the information he had just given me, not the skin he had just revealed. He'd owned this house for five years, and there was nothing personal anywhere. No marker that it was anything different than one of the many hotel suites they had stayed in together.

"Dinner should be ready for us."

"Is it dinnertime?"

It felt like morning to me. But I realized that I had been awake for twenty-four hours, changed time zones during that time, slept for about six hours, then changed time zones again.

Time, at this point, truly was relative.

"It is dinner hour, but you may call it whatever you wish."

For a moment I thought it was significant we were sharing a meal. And then I realized we had done so many times. But we had never sat down to a table together. It had never been officially having dinner, going on a date or anything like that. We had eaten together in bed. Countless times.

In many ways, we shared a lot more intimacy than I had given us credit for.

He knew what my favorite thing to get from room service was.

He didn't know what I would order at a restaurant, though.

And that highlighted just how turned inside out our intimacies were.

He walked ahead of me, and I followed, since I didn't know where anything in the house was. He led me into the dining room, where there was a massive, long table with candles flickering in candelabras. Food was spread from one end to the other, as if he had been expecting a dinner party, and not just me.

"Not exactly a cheeseburger," I said, looking at the potatoes, steak and glorious roasted vegetables, along with the basket of rolls and platter of cheese and meat set out on the table.

"If you would rather have a cheeseburger, then I can call the staff back."

"This will do," I said, doing my best to keep my tone dry.

I was learning about a third version of Hades, I realized.

Whatever this was. I didn't think it was the real him. But then the real him wasn't the man that I saw in different business meetings either. Not entirely.

The closest thing, I really did think, was the man who took me to bed, but even that man had secrets.

More than I had even begun to guess at.

"What is this exactly?"

"Dinner," he said, his voice hard. He sat down at the head of the table, as if he expected me to take a seat at his right hand. To be spiteful, I sat at his left, with one chair space between us.

"I can see that it's dinner," I said. "But I'm not entirely certain what farce this is. We know each other far too well to engage in this kind of behavior. You can't pretend to be civilized with me, Hades. I know who you are. I know what you like. You pretend. Every day you pretend. And when you first get the chance, you come to my room, to my bed, and you tie me to it. You're not civilized. Any more than I am."

"Do you want to live that way? Because I don't. I lived with a father who didn't bother to engage in civility in his daily life. Better, I think, to have an outlet for it in the bedroom, than to leave it all over the dining table, don't you think?"

I could understand what he was saying. He was equating the passion between us to the abuse his father had meted out, and that wasn't fair. What we did was intense, but it wasn't abusive. We both wanted it. We both enjoyed it. No one was a victim of anything. He knew that, I knew he did. If he thought for even one second that what he did might cause me harm, he simply would never… He would never.

"Eat," he said.

I would have loved to shout back at him that I wasn't hungry. Sadly, I was. The nausea had begun to shift into peckishness, and I found that I really did want something to eat.

"You were going to marry Jessica Clare, and… Never sleep with her?"

"Of course I intended to sleep with her. I intended to sleep with her and produce children."

"But you wouldn't have slept with her until then."

"I didn't especially want her," he said. "However, I am a goal-oriented man and, given a reason, I could have roused myself to do so."

I looked down at my food, my lip curling. "I see."

"Did you never have plans to marry?"

I frowned. "No. I did. At least, I hoped to someday. I hoped to find someone that was nothing like you. A man who would give me a gentle, easy life. Who would support my ambitions. Who would… Be nothing like either my mother or my father. Someone I can have a partnership with."

His black eyes were fathomless. His lips flat. "How cozy."

"Does it sound cozy?" I looked around the stark space. "If this is your version of *cozy*, Hades, we have a long way to go."

"Sweet summer child. My version of *cozy* is the underworld. Or hadn't you figured that out yet? This is me attempting to be human." He smiled, but it wasn't nice. "I had thought that you might like it better."

I couldn't tell if he was being dry, if he was exaggerating to prove a point, or if he was actually being sadly, extremely honest.

But that was the problem. I knew compartmentalized, masked versions of him.

And he knew the same of me.

"I'm still not sure what the performance is. We got married with an hour of planning. I found out I was pregnant… It hasn't even been a day. I am exhausted. I can't even begin to picture… To picture what the future looks like. A child, Hades. You and me."

I didn't think I imagined that his skin went slightly waxen then. "We will hire professionals," he said. "People to care for the child who are experts in development, and in psychology."

"You think that's what the child needs?"

"I know what a child does not need. I know what my father did to me was…" He looked off into the distance. "He made me into an exceptional businessman. He made me into a weapon. I have one weakness. That has proven to be you. Over and over again. Oddly, it is the weakness I find more concerning than any of the emotionless strengths. Because at least when it comes to other areas of my life I can act dispassionately. With you it's never dispassionate."

I didn't know whether to be flattered by that or not. And because this wasn't a few stolen hours. Because this was our life. Our relationship. Our future. I decided to just go ahead and say it. "Is that a compliment? You keep talking about me like I'm a venereal disease that you can't get rid of. There aren't antibiotics strong enough to rid you of Florence Clare."

"You speak of me as if I'm the same."

I knew that was true. I wasn't any more flattering to him than he was to me. I only knew how to talk about the thing between us in a way that could protect me.

If I spoke of it like it was a sickness, something that was being done to me, something that I didn't want, then somehow I wasn't at fault for it. And perhaps couldn't be hurt by it. But when he had said that he was getting married, it had been proven to me that I could be quite hurt by it. I was far too vulnerable with him.

But if he was ever going to change…

No one had ever made him feel safe. No one had ever shown him what a family should look like. I wasn't sure I had a lock on that, but maybe I could… show him.

"This is something I never wanted to do to you," he said. "Do you want honesty? I am the son of a black hole. A man who absorbed and destroyed everything that came into his sphere. I never wanted to put you in a position where my hand would be in your business, but here we are. It is how we must go. I never wanted to put you in a position where your life would be directly connected with mine."

"You should have thought of that before you took my virginity, Hades. Because our lives have been bound together ever since, and you know that."

"Sex, Florence. And for a while that's what it was. And it was fine. We took risks. That day, a risk that… Had its reward, I suppose. Now we must figure out what to do with it. But you act as if you want something else from me than this." He swept his hand along the distance of the table. "From a nice dinner, from a warm dwelling. How? And why? Because this is not temporary. Nor is it a few stolen hours. We must think about what we can maintain. What can be sustained."

Was he worried? About us drowning in desire for each other now that we had an endless amount of time?

I looked at him, and I honestly couldn't say.

He was a man who made little sense to me.

My feelings for him made little sense to me.

He was like a puzzle that I could never quite put together. I had been a foolish girl but I was eighteen. I had looked at him and seen myself. The child of a powerful man, who didn't have his mother around. Who had been dragged to all of these events. Who wanted to do well. Who had a sense of exceptionalism. I had looked at him and I thought I had found the other side to myself.

Or maybe it was something I had convinced myself of so that I could justify wanting to sleep with him.

But we weren't the same. I had been telling myself we were all this time. But while this experience was showing me where I was vulnerable, where I was soft, he was doubling down on artifice.

And wanting me to thank him for it.

I wondered then how we would handle it if what had happened was a one-night stand. If we didn't actually assume that we knew each other. If it wasn't the product of ten years' worth of risky behavior that had finally caught us out.

But if we had been true strangers, rather than this…strange thing that we were. Strangers who had watched each other brush their teeth.

Strangers who knew each other's room service order by heart.

Something had to give.

He couldn't.

Maybe it would have to be me.

"When I was little," I said, "I thought my mother was the most beautiful woman in the world. I used to love to watch her get ready to go out. Once, I told my father that. He laughed at me. He asked me if I had ever read a newspaper. He asked why I didn't know that when my mother went out it was to humiliate him. He said that she was a whore, and that everything beautiful she put on her face and everything lovely she wrapped her body in were lures to catch men like they were unsuspecting large-mouthed bass." I flinched inside, even thinking of it. It had been such an unnecessary thing to say to a child. I had loved both my father and mother so much. I loved my father all the way up to the end, even knowing that he was flawed. Even knowing that in that moment his hurt had allowed him to be so unkind.

I swallowed hard. "All I knew then was that I could never be like my mother. Not really. I had wanted to be. What little girl wouldn't? She is quite simply one of the most stunning women in the world. And maybe now she has changed. Some of it was too much plastic surgery, but isn't that the mark of pain for a woman who has spent her life being defined by a certain sort of beauty? All I know is in that moment I was taught to fear beauty. I was taught there was something cynical, dangerous, beneath that sort of femininity."

I leaned back in my chair. "Then I looked up the articles on my mother. Like he suggested. I was eight, maybe. Reading about how my mother was suspected of having multiple affairs. Do you know, until that moment I hadn't realized that the older boys who came around sometimes were my half brothers? You probably know Javier and Rocco better than I do. My father actually wasn't cruel. Not habitually. He made mistakes. He certainly said the wrong things out of anger. Even without the intent of being cruel, he took my view of the world and twisted it. He made me afraid of being a woman. Because when I saw the things that they wrote about her, I knew I never wanted that to be me. It will be now, don't you think?"

I shook my head and laughed. "Here I am, her daughter. Felled by the absolutely wrong man. By my inability to resist desire. Temptation. Caught in a snare of my own beauty."

He stared at me, his eyes blank. "And why are you telling me this?"

"Because you don't know it. Because for all these years, for all of this… History between us. We don't know each other. We can't sit down and strategize what kind of marriage we are going to have like we are having a business meeting. We have to actually make allowances for the people that we are. Maybe we even need to get to know each other."

"Do you even know yourself, Florence?"

The words were like a slap, directly across my face.

"Excuse me?"

"You strike me as one of the most disingenuous people on the planet. You wear a mask all the time. The only place that I have ever found you to be remotely authentic is when you're naked. On your knees. Tied to a bed. Then I see glimpses of who you might be. You go into business meetings like you are dressed for war."

I flinched, because it was nothing less than the truth. Except… I did know myself. I did. I understood why I turned away from the things that I wanted. Why I forced myself to be a specific kind of strong, because I had decided that being soft was too weak.

I understood that I had decided to pattern my life more after my father because…

Because I would be more successful. Because I didn't want to be an object of ridicule. Yes, my mother had monetary success. She was famous. But not for the things that I wanted to be famous for.

So the only other way that I could even begin to

think to find success wasn't behaving like my father. I knew that I did that.

And when I went home, I… Worked more. I went out for drinks with my friend, and I didn't tell her that I had an obsession with my business rival, because…

Because the real things about myself embarrassed me.

Because the truth of me was something that not even I wanted to know.

And that he saw that, while he remained an enigma to me, made me so angry I wanted to pick up my plate and throw it in his face.

"What makes you so confident that I am myself with you?" I asked.

"Because you have no reason to perform. You never wanted anything from me but my body, and that means you are an exceptionally honest lover. You only take what you want. And nothing more. And everything you give is something that you want to give. It is not an insult."

"No. Just the idea that I don't know my own mind."

"Am I wrong?" he asked.

"What about you? Who are you, really? You're not any better than I am. You were looking to style a marriage to keep your business. You have no heart. No soul."

"Ah, but the difference between you and I is I don't believe that I do."

"No, the difference between you and I is that I do. You will recall my reaction to your engagement."

His face went blank. "Yes. I do recall that. If nothing else, Florence, I do enjoy your passion."

Something about that sent me over the edge. An edge I couldn't see the bottom of. I found myself standing up, moving over to where he sat at the head of the table. He turned toward me, looking up, his eyes glittering.

I was trying to find something new between us. But this was…familiar. This was us.

Our connection.

Maybe I could find something new in it.

I reached behind my back and unzipped my dress. Letting it fall to my waist, down to the floor.

I had succeeded in shocking him. I could see it on his face then.

He had not expected that.

I took off my bra, pushed my panties down and stepped out of my shoes.

Then I maneuvered myself so that I was straddling his lap, completely naked, while he sat there fully clothed.

I gripped his face in my hands, and I kissed him. Not the performance that we had engaged in at the church, for the paparazzi. But a kiss for him, a kiss for me. A kiss to prove to him that I was not cold-blooded. Not in any capacity.

"Why?" he asked, gripping hold of my hands, taking them captive.

"I don't know how to talk to you," I said, because that was honest. Because it revealed something, when normally I never would have. But this had to be us and new all at the same time. I would find a way. "But I have more than enough practice wanting you. Whether I'm angry with you, whether I think I hate you, or not. And I'm tired. I am so tired of living in all these moments that I don't know how to handle. I want you. Because at least I understand that. I've had years to come to terms with it. There is no logic in it. There is nothing right about it. But it simply is. And I need something that makes sense."

He growled, wrapped his arm around my waist and stood, moving his other hand to my thigh, bracing me as he carried me away from the dining table and down the vast hall toward the bedroom. The lights came on automatically as we entered the room, and he deposited me in the center of the bed.

I watched him hungrily as he began to undo the buttons on that white shirt.

As he began to expose his gorgeous chest, a feast for my eyes that I would never tire of.

He moved his hand to his belt, undoing it with one hand, then he untucked the shirt and shrugged it from his shoulders, depositing it on the floor. He slid his belt from the loops, but did not bind me with it this time. Instead, it went down with the shirt, followed by everything else. Until his gloriously familiar body was pressed against mine. Naked and perfect and everything that I had ever desired.

He looked down into my eyes, and he kissed me. It was familiar, and yet…

It was our wedding night.

It was our wedding night.

I could not push that thought away once I had it.

This wasn't the same. It wasn't a few stolen moments in a hotel room. An hour between meetings.

This was our wedding night.

Hades was no longer my dirty secret. And I was no longer his.

He was my husband. I was his wife.

And it was like he could read those thoughts moving through my mind, because something changed. In the way he held me, in the way he kissed me. It was still desperate.

But there was… Something else in it that I couldn't put a name to.

Like the tone of the desperation had changed. As if the melody of the song had shifted.

His tongue slid against mine, claiming me deep. And I clung to his shoulders, broad and magnificent. I moved my hands down his back, gloried in those familiar muscles.

This wasn't the last time.

That thought stabbed me. Made tears prick my eyes.

It wasn't the last time.

Every other time it had felt like it might be. Had felt like it had the potential to be.

In the time when we had conceived the baby…

I had been so sure that it was a goodbye I wasn't ready to have.

I'd given one that had felt necessary. One that had felt like the right thing. Except it had torn me to pieces.

But this wasn't the last time.

This was the first night of something else. Something different, if we could find a way to make it work.

Yes, I had done the familiar thing by kissing him. Perhaps taking him to bed had, in the moment, felt like the easy thing.

This wasn't easy, though.

It never had been.

It had always been a fight for something. For something that didn't have a name.

For a satisfaction that might never see its end.

Just like I had realized there was strength in softness as I made my way up to the head of the altar at the church, I realized there was more to this than I had ever let myself believe.

The sex was a conversation. In a way that I had not ever let myself understand.

His hands spoke volumes as they moved over my skin.

Whether it was rough or soft.

His mouth, commanding, soft, cruel, caring, could speak without words.

He kissed his way down my body, forced my legs apart and licked me directly at my center.

His tongue over my slick flesh was hot, perfect. And I arched my hips up against him, grabbed his head and held him there as he feasted on me like he would never get enough.

He wasn't sorry that he had married me.

That was another strange and clarifying thought.

This was not a man who wanted another woman.

He would've slept with her. That wounded me.

But he… He hadn't wanted her. It would never have been this.

Not ever.

Maybe he really didn't have this with anyone else.

Because this was singular. This was him, and it was me. And maybe he had been right about that too.

That this was the most myself I ever was. In his arms. Because it was the only place I could actually be soft. The only place I wasn't afraid of what I wanted. The only place I wasn't scared of my own pleasure.

I had been wounded, thinking about how I was the one person he never had to worry would sell stories about him. But it occurred to me that I had often felt safest with him for that very reason.

He could not betray me without betraying himself.

And so we had real trust. Real safety between us and I had never truly appreciated why. Or how deep it ran.

He pushed two fingers inside of me and I reached my peak, crying out his name until he moved up my body and kissed me again, swallowing my pleasure whole.

Then he thrust inside of me in one, smooth movement. I lost my breath.

I held his face in my hands, and he pressed his forehead to mine as he began to move.

As he claimed me. Possessed me.

"Hades," I whispered against his mouth.

He growled, his movements becoming a frenzy.

I felt desire begin to build in me again, higher and higher, harder and faster.

We were a storm. Fire. Destruction. Everything bad that I had ever labeled us.

But we were something else too.

Even if I couldn't find a name for it.

His pleasure unraveled him, as he shook and found his peak, gripping my hips as he poured himself into me. And I found my own oblivion, biting his neck to keep from saying his name again. Because I could only strip myself bare so many times.

Afterward, as the oblivion cleared, I realized that we had nowhere to run to.

Because he was my husband. I was his wife.

And I was in love with him.

# CHAPTER TEN

After that I couldn't sleep. He did. And deeply. Which struck me as the most infuriatingly male thing that had ever occurred.

I loved him, though.

And I found myself sitting up by the window, gazing thoughtlessly out into the darkness at what I knew was the vast expanse of wilderness below.

Hades was like that wilderness. I had been looking at the trees and not beyond. Into the darkness. At the vastness contained there.

This revelation made me rethink everything. From that very first moment. Because if I evaluated the things that I had done through a lens of feeling, rather than simple lust, I saw him differently.

If I took the things that he had just told me, and I mixed them with the realization that had just come from my own heart, then I saw things differently.

That first time. When I had invited him to the hotel room. What had he been thinking? Had he been worried about the consequences if his father were to find out that we met? Did he think that I had been about to ask him corporate secrets? Or had he known from the beginning that we were going to…

I had never asked him. We needed to talk. That was one of the very simple truths that I stumbled upon over the course of the night.

We had to stop defaulting to sex, because that was easy for us.

I had convinced myself that we had no intimacy. That wasn't true. But we had gaps in our intimacy.

Like knowing each other's room service order, but not what we like to have at a regular dinner.

I knew a strange, vacation version of him, as he did of me.

And we needed to build a home together. That was the way that we were going to find the parts of each other we hadn't seen before. That was the only way that I was going to get to know the man behind the mask.

He was so determined to make rules. I didn't agree with that. I didn't agree with the concept. I wanted something that felt more real.

But he was the way that he was. Which meant we weren't going to fall into that. Not accidentally. I was going to have to do something.

I had started this.

I was going to have to keep pushing to change it.

I finally slept, for a couple of fitful hours, though I didn't sleep beside him. I opted to curl up on the chaise by the window. Mostly because I didn't trust myself. Mostly because I knew if given half the chance, I would make love to him again. Because I wanted to. Because I loved him.

The sex last night had been different. Maybe because I knew I loved him.

Maybe because we were married.

I considered that as I brooded over a cup of coffee far too early.

He came out for a moment, shirtless, stunning.

"Thank you for the coffee," he said. As he poured some from the coffee maker.

"It was a byproduct of my own need for caffeine."

I smiled. He looked surprised by my expression.

"What?" I asked.

"I thought you were mad at me."

I shook my head. "No. I'm not. I was thinking, though. About our first time together."

He cleared his throat and leaned against the counter. The muscles in his torso shifted, and I found myself powerless to look away.

"One of my favorite memories," he said.

This felt like the sort of bubble we often found ourselves in after long nights in hotels. Where we were too tired, too satisfied to keep our guard up. When he would smile like it didn't hurt him to do it. And I would tell him a story about my friends. When he'd tell me about his time at university—the one moment when he hadn't always been serious—and he'd done fantastically dangerous stunts like leaping from yachts with his friends. And for a moment, we would be like this. Just us. No businesses, no shields. I wondered what it would take to get us here all the time.

Because this was what I was in love with. These moments. The spaces.

Liar. You love him when he's intense too.

Well. That was true. I couldn't actually separate all the different versions of him that I knew. I couldn't say that I loved one and not the other. He was complicated. And I was beginning to realize I loved him even in his complication. Perhaps because of it.

"Is it?"

"Yes. I thought all my dreams had come true."

Those words felt fragile. Like if I moved too quickly, spoke too quickly, they would evaporate. And there would be no evidence that they had ever been there.

"I was curious what you thought initially. When I sent you the note. When I asked you to meet me."

"I… Of course, being a man, I thought perhaps you wanted me. But then I thought perhaps it was also wishful thinking."

I looked at him, avidly. Hungrily. I wanted to know what he was thinking now. What he'd been thinking then. Sometimes I felt like I wanted to slip beneath his skin and inhabit him entirely. So that I could finally know him.

Would I ever know him?

"Wishful thinking, what do you mean by that?" I asked.

He lifted a brow. "You're not naive, Florence. Come on now."

"Maybe I'm not naive, not in general. But there are

things about you that I have never been able to figure out, Hades. So maybe I just need you to tell me."

He looked mystified. A crease forming on his forehead. I wanted to smooth it, but I also wanted to analyze his every muscle movement to try and glean more information. So I didn't smooth any of it away.

"You must know that I wanted you for…" He shook his head. "An inappropriately long time. I met you, and there had never been anybody like you. You infuriated me. You are so opinionated. My father hated your father, and that made you…"

"Forbidden," I whispered.

He nodded slowly. "Yes."

"I thought that. That perhaps I wanted you so badly because you were the one thing I really couldn't have."

He leaned just a bit closer. "And what was your conclusion?"

I shrugged. "But it doesn't matter why. Because it's real either way and there's nothing I can do about it."

"Fatalistic." He moved away slightly, some of our tension broken.

"I think both of us are entirely fatalistic in the approach to our affair, don't you?"

"Perhaps. But yes. I think you were sixteen the first time I noticed that you were beautiful. But I set you at a distance for obvious reasons. I was too old for you."

"And my birthday magically fixed that?"

He paused for a moment, as if considering. Thinking.

"No. It didn't. When you were eighteen you were still too young for me. But you made plain what had been secret before, and once you told me you wanted me I wasn't going to turn you away."

"So you hoped that I was going to try to seduce you?"

"Yes," he bit out. "Because I never would have seduced you. I would never have touched you, for so many reasons. It was the wrong thing to do, even with you being insistent it was what you wanted. It was the wrong thing to do. I knew it. But the attraction that burned between us was uncommon. Then and always."

"Yes. It was."

I couldn't help but smile. He wanted me. It had felt inevitable to him, as it did to me. Or we had been lying to ourselves because we want it so badly. Whatever the answer was, whether it was fate, or a lack of desire to resist, it didn't matter to me. Because it boiled down to the fact that I wasn't alone.

That it hadn't only been me burning.

"Afterward, what did you think?"

He laughed. Hard and bitter. "When we left the resort, I was determined that I would never touch you again. After that weekend, when I made you mine in every way possible. I was… I should not have treated you that way."

"What way? Like a woman who wanted some incredibly hot sex and got it?"

"I should not have treated you like a woman with experience."

"I certainly walked away from that weekend a woman with experience," I said, smiling softly.

"You were a virgin. And I gave no quarter for that."

"You certainly ruined me. In the sense that I could never have wanted anything more mundane afterward." I was quiet for a moment. "Why did you come for me again? The second time? If you were determined not to…"

"I will never be able to say. Why you test my control when it is something I have always otherwise found so easy to keep hold of. Why… It was like you fundamentally changed something in me. Before you, I had never set a foot out of line. Before you, I had never defied my father because of the sword he had dangling over my head. The safety of my mother. I was angry. I was… Well, you saw. Everything that you saw in me as a young man, that was my simmering rage at my father. But I never let it out. Not around him. I never let anything off leash. And then there was you. You touched me, and you kissed me. And I was powerless to do anything but take what you had on offer. To show you exactly what our bodies could do together. And then in Switzerland…"

I realized then that we were in Switzerland. What a funny thing. Our second time together had been in Geneva. At that glorious hotel with all the high-gloss marble. He had me in the bathroom.

I looked up at him, and I knew that we were in the middle of a shared memory. His eyes burned.

And in that fire I saw so much.

This was so much of him, a look behind a normally locked door. I didn't want him to close it, I felt panicky at the thought. I was hungry for him. More of him. All of him I could have.

"Geneva," I said.

He pushed away from the counter and walked out of the kitchen. I followed him. He was standing there with his back to me, facing the vast wilderness below. "Geneva is just there," he said, pointing to lights that I could only just barely see beyond the fabric of the mountains. "When I looked down there, I always think of that. Of us. In Geneva. Of the moment that you walked in, wearing some lovely, floral dress. Nothing like what you are now. It was very soft. And you looked impossibly beautiful. I had been drowning in my need for you for those months. I wished… So much, that I could find a woman and ease the ache inside of me, but I could not force myself to want anybody else. I went out. I had drinks. I couldn't force myself to lose control when you weren't there. And then the minute you were there… It was like the fabric that made up the core of my being torn apart. Six months without sex, Florence. And I grabbed hold of your hand and took you into a bathroom and… I behaved like an animal."

I was trying to process all of this. The revelation that he hadn't been with anybody in those months between our first time and our second.

"I love that," I said. "I thought it was the most glorious… Romantic…"

"Taking you on the bathroom counter was hardly romantic."

"It was to me. Because I had done nothing but think

about you. I made myself ill with it, Hades. I had tried to tell myself that you would have forgotten me thirty times over by the time we ever saw one another again, and that we were never going to touch, let alone kiss, let alone make love. And then I saw you and the fire was just as hot as it ever was. We never have been able to put it out. I can't even express what a relief it was when you kissed me. When you locked me in that room. When you stripped me naked. When your skin was on mine. I had never wanted anything quite so badly as I wanted that. Hades, I wanted it. More than you'll ever know."

He looked away from me, and I studied his profile. There were so many things I did not understand about this man. But I knew that we were in a house in Switzerland with a view of Geneva, and he thought of me when he looked out that window. I knew that I loved him.

That he was my husband, that we were having a baby.

That this was forever, and would not be the scattered, passionate encounters that had fueled us for so long.

Things had changed, and we could not behave the same.

"I have to work," he said. "We need to get press releases ready. I have paperwork to review from my lawyer."

"I'll need to look at it too," I said.

"Florence, let me. Let me start this. You rest. You're pregnant," he said.

Hearing him acknowledge it, in a way that wasn't just him railing about me having his baby, but about my actual condition and his concern for it, made me feel something warm.

"All right," I said. Because at some point I was going to have to let my guard down. At some point I was going to have to trust him. I cared so much about the company. And yet, it wasn't the sole source of my identity. That had never been clearer. I was having a baby. I had married Hades. Making it the sole source of my identity was half my problem. It had made it so that I couldn't fully see myself. Hades had been right. I didn't know my own heart.

I loved him.

I loved fighting with him in the business arena because I loved having his attention. Because I loved having him look at me. Because I liked showing him that I was good at my job.

Because I wanted him to think so too.

I wanted him to respect me.

My father was gone. The only other person in the whole world whose opinion mattered even half so much was Hades.

I wasn't going to examine that too closely, but I was determined to make changes.

To fill in our gaps. I made some phone calls, and arranged for Christmas decorations to be brought to the chalet. Along with an extremely elaborate dinner.

I was going to make this a home. Because we needed to become a family. We were something. We had been from the beginning. I understood now that for me it was love.

I couldn't say what it was for him. Powerful, certainly. He made it sound like an illness, and in fairness, I had often felt like that's what it was.

But maybe that was how love unnamed felt. Love without boundaries and security. Unspoken. Uncertain.

Now suddenly that I found a place for it, something to call it, now that I was his wife, it felt less like a sickness and much more like peace.

I had no real idea how our marriage was going to unfold or what kind of husband he was going to be. But I knew that for the six months between our first and second encounter he hadn't been with another woman.

He had said that I wouldn't want him to be faithful to me because I wouldn't want to be the focus of all of his desire, and yet… It seemed that even when I wasn't with him, ten years ago, I had been the sole focus of his desire.

That he couldn't manufacture it for somebody else. And he hadn't slept with Jessica.

It was a question I didn't really want to ask, because it felt unrealistic to assume…

But perhaps I was not the only one who couldn't find it in them to take another lover. Perhaps I wasn't the only one who would rather be celibate than with somebody I wanted less.

By the time Hades was done with his meeting, I had the entire house bedecked. It glittered with decorations of champagne and gold. It went with the minimalistic Norwegian design all around, but added glitter. Sparkle.

Maybe this would begin to show him what I wanted. What I felt.

He looked around, completely stunned.

"What is this?"

"Christmas," I said. "Because we are going to be a family."

He looked at me, and the expression on his face was like shock. "And why would Christmas matter?"

He'd said that Christmas had been used as a weapon against him.

"Because we get to choose who we'll be," I said. "I spent Christmas split between houses. It wasn't a weapon in the way your dad used it, but it often felt fraught to me. I don't want our child to have that experience. Our family will be different."

"Family?"

"Yes. We're having a baby. And… I understand why that scares you. I understand why you think we need nannies and psychologists, and I'm not opposed to any of those things if you think that it would help. But I think that we can find family between the two of us. Because there is so much between us, Hades, and I truly believe that we can spin it into something lovely. We are not our families. We are making a new one."

This felt like a gambit. The kind of risk I normally took in the boardroom, not in my personal life. But nothing mattered more than this. If I couldn't make this work, if I couldn't find my way with him, what future was there?

This wasn't a contract. No merger or business deal. It was only our whole lives.

"Florence…"

"I made dinner. I mean, I called and had dinner delivered."

I took his hand and led him into the dining room. It was not set with a massive spread that would allow us to have distance between each other. Just one corner of the table, with bread and meats and cheeses. The chairs pushed up together. "Talk to me," I said.

"I have been talking all day," he said. "Making sure that we do this legally is complicated."

"Tell me about it. All of it. Because we are no longer hiding our business dealings from one another."

So he did. And I felt myself falling in love with him all over again, because what was sexier than listening to this man talk about business? Businesses we both cared about, things that we both loved.

"I really would love to be involved in the super ship," I said.

"You really like the cruise ships?"

"I love them," I said. "The ocean just feels so free to me. I love the idea of being able to feel at home while you travel. And I just loved the adventure of it."

"You are secretly quite intrepid."

I looked down. "I suppose I am. I always tried to shut the wilder parts of myself down, because they reminded my father of my mother. And… You know how he felt about her."

"It was unfair of him to say all those things to you."

"I agree," I said. "But I think it made me a better CEO. Except… I don't know. In the end I got pregnant with your baby, so maybe it didn't. Maybe it had to find other ways to leak out. In my love of the ocean and my love of jumping on you whenever I had a spare moment."

Humor gleamed in his eyes, and I felt proud of that. "You're brilliant, you know," I said.

A crease appeared between his brows, and something that looked like a smile stretched his lips. It was the oddest expression. "Thank you?"

"I'm serious. You know, I have often thought that I enjoyed fighting with you so much because nobody else really feels a challenge. I really appreciate the fact that sometimes you're better than me. Not always. But sometimes. It's nice to know that I can lose."

"I suppose I like that about you too," he said slowly. "I don't like to lose."

"But have you ever lost anyone else?"

"No," he said.

I wanted to ask him if he had ever… Since us… But those words stuck in my throat, because I felt vulnerable about the whole thing. About what my answer would be.

But then… What was the point of holding back? I was sitting there surrounded by Christmas decorations I had procured, having dinner with the father of my baby. A man who knew my body better than I did. And I was embarrassed to tell him that he was my only lover?

Or maybe I was just afraid of finding out that it had never been as special to him as it was to me.

"There's never been anyone else," I said. Because I decided to lead with my own vulnerability. As much as I hated it.

Because that wasn't something either my mother or father ever would've done. They were so committed to their roles. To the characters that they played. My mother to her daft socialite persona, which kept everybody from getting too close to her. My father to his steely businessman facade. Neither could admit that they were wrong. Neither could open a vein, not even if they chose to. So my mother was forever creating arterial spray that would do Hollywood proud. It was a facade. A ruse. I wasn't going to continue on that pattern.

We had to break our patterns.

For all the reasons that I had just said to him, we could be a family in a different way.

I was going to have to lead by example.

"What?" He looked fierce suddenly.

"You know that I've never touched another man. Never kissed one. I wanted you, from the first moment that I ever saw you, and I told myself… When I planned on maybe marrying someone else, I had hoped that perhaps I could find somebody that I felt half of what I felt for you. A man who made me burn only half as bright, I thought that seemed reasonable. But I couldn't even find that. I dreamed of you in between."

He looked past me, at the wall.

"There've been no other women, Florence. Not since we were together the first time. I might not have been a virgin the first time we came together, but I have not touched anyone since."

It was so huge an admission I almost couldn't take it on board. It made me want to weep. So I sidestepped. I wasn't proud, but it was easier to focus on something that had wounded me than on whatever this deep emotion in me was.

"You were going to," I said, accusing.

"I felt I had no other choice. I wanted… I lied to you. On the plane. I told you that I thought you would simply not be able to resist me. I did think that you would. I thought you would be so angry with me, so disgusted that I was married, that you would never touch me again. I thought that it would set us both free, Florence, and that was what I wanted."

I felt like I'd been stabbed. He had wanted me to go away. He had wanted to end this.

"Then why didn't you just end it?"

"If I was strong enough to end it…"

I knew the answer. I already did. Because it was the answer that we both always came back to. If we could stop, we could stop. If we could be finished, we would be finished.

If we could save ourselves from this, we would.

So he had hoped that he had put up a wall so tall that I wouldn't want to scale it.

"You are one of the most moral and upright people I know," he said. "There is nothing shadowy about you. I knew you would never touch a married man."

"And then I had the bad luck of getting pregnant." Tears filled my eyes. "Hades, I wish that I could tell you your plan would've worked. I have never been quite so—" I avoided the word *heartbroken*. "When I found out about the engagement I was sick. Because I imagined you sleeping with her just after you left me. I imagined you touching her just before you came to me. But it was jealousy. It wasn't moral outrage in the way that I wished it could be. I tried to fashion it into moral outrage. I tried to tell myself I was hurt for her. Because she didn't know what you were.

"But I was hurt for me. And when I went into your office to yell at you, I didn't even consider resisting you. I am afraid that it would've continued that way."

Something in his expression was tortured then. But in a breath it was gone, and it had been so singular that I couldn't quite remember it as it was. Couldn't sit there and pull it apart and try to put names to each and every flicker of emotion that had crossed his face then. I felt robbed. Robbed of the moment when I could have tried to understand him. Just a little more. Just a little better.

"The pregnancy made the decision for us. This is not something…" He shook his head. "I did not want to trap you in this."

"The merger?"

He looked at me. "Yes. The merger. But now… Now here we are."

"You will be faithful to me," I said.

Because now it was clear that he would be, because he always had been.

"If you ever wish it to be different, just say so. If you ever regret any of this…"

How can I regret it? I had never wanted another man the way that I wanted him.

I loved him. And I wanted to spend this time we had away showing him.

"Hades, do you know what we've never done?"

"What is that?"

"We've never been on a date."

# CHAPTER ELEVEN

IT TOOK SEVERAL days for Hades to be able to come up for air after dealing with all the legality of the merger.

We signed off on the paperwork extremely late on the fourth day, and that was when he told me he had a surprise for me.

"I will take you out tomorrow," he said.

"It's not even Christmas yet," I said.

"I know," he said. "But I was thinking about what you said. We have not been on a date."

The last few days had been strange for us. We had sex, but we had managed to talk quite a bit in between. And do work. I was right; we needed to fill in those gaps. And we were. Much more competently than I had expected us to.

We had breakfast together. Lunch. Dinner.

We moved in the rhythm of each other's life. Rather than existing in stolen fragments of time.

It was that shot of intensity, but with everything in between.

I liked him. And that was an interesting thing. I had realized I loved him first. But it still felt very sharp.

A bit uneasy.

But I liked everything about him. Well, not all of his mercurial moods, not while they were happening, but I didn't think that he would be him without them.

Because without them, he wouldn't be intense. And I did love the intensity. Especially when it was all focused on me.

I liked the way he talked about business. I like the way it felt to sit next to him. I like him as much as I ever thought that I had hated him, and that was saying something.

But I had only ever been protecting myself. That much was clear.

I had only been able to make space for myself to love the company, because I thought that I had to succeed at that or everything else would fall apart. Or I wouldn't matter. Or I would be my mother. I couldn't see a middle ground. But that, in and of itself, was flawed thinking.

It didn't let me be a whole person. And I really badly needed to figure out how to be a whole person.

I could love my job—I did love it. But I could also love myself.

I didn't need to be subsumed.

Because I had lived with people who had become parodies of themselves, and that kept you from being what you needed to be for the children depending on you. I knew that well.

It also didn't help a marriage. And my marriage to Hades meant a lot to me. So much.

I opened up the closet when it was time for us to get ready for dinner and gasped at what I saw.

There was a gold dress inside that glittered like all the Christmas decorations I had bought for the house.

It was so deliberate, it had to be intentional.

"Hades," I breathed.

"I want badly to see you in that," he said. He moved over to me, kissed my neck and wrapped his arm around me, his chest hot against my back. "More, though, I want to take it off of you."

"That can be arranged," I whispered. "Maybe we can make it like old times. Find a coat closet."

He growled. "I'm done with coat closets. You're mine. And I'm going to show the world that you're mine. Then I'll take you home to our bed, where I will stretch you out and feast on you like I have all the time in the world. Because I do."

Nothing could have been sexier. But then, that was how he was. Nothing could be sexier than him.

We had to take a helicopter down the mountain, and I clung to him again as we did so, but this time I didn't resent it, or him.

"Geneva," I whispered, as the glittering city came into view.

"Good memories," he said.

"Yes," I whispered.

A car was there to pick us up after the helicopter landed on the edge of town, and whisked us to a glorious restaurant in an old palace. If people were staring at us, I didn't care. Because for the first time, I was out in public with him.

For the first time…

Yes. There had been headlines and all kinds of

things about our wedding, about our kissing. There had been a storm. But I had ignored it because I was with him. And when I was with him nothing else really mattered.

Now we were out together, making something new. Something we had never experienced before.

It was amazing how much had changed in the past two months, but then, also how nothing had changed.

It was like the hard knot of my feelings that had lived in this deep place inside of me had been given room to grow and expand. So that I could finally see what they were trying to become all along.

It was always supposed to be love. For me, that was always what it was supposed to be.

I still couldn't quite figure it out with him, though, and I didn't want to disrupt what we were building.

I had to be patient. Though, patience had never been my particular strong suit.

I was, after all, the same person who had seduced Hades on my eighteenth birthday, because I hadn't been able to wait another second.

But now I would have to wait. We had all the trust in the world in each other's bodies. But the rest of it… We didn't have practice with it. Not yet.

I was trying to figure out how to learn this. How to learn him.

How to get over the walls inside of him.

Or maybe it wasn't walls so much as a series of locked doors and different rooms. Sometimes he let me into one room, but it closed off another. I could never access all of him all at once.

He had shared some things, but it always felt like it was being dragged from him. And there was more. I could feel it. He could be so remote, so hard. And yet he was so passionate too. I wanted to feel the passion. All of it. Always.

I wanted everything.

I let him order for us.

“I like it,” I said.

“What?”

“Letting you make decisions for me sometimes. I’m exhausted. From deciding everything all the time.” I looked at him. “What can I do for you?”

He raised his brows. “You already do it.”

He meant sex. And that was not particularly flattering or romantic, but I can understand how he meant it. Because for him, that was maybe when he was his most honest.

“I am always happy to accommodate,” I said.

But I determined that I was going to figure out a way to make moments in his life better. Not just naked moments.

I became aware after our plates were put in front of us that we were drawing a bit of attention.

I looked up at him and moved my eyes to the left, knowing his gaze would follow. And it did. There were two girls giggling and raising their phones, clearly taking video or photos of us.

“You know,” I said softly. “At one time, that would have been my worst nightmare.”

“Yes,” he said. “I know.”

"You know why, though. It was never because I was ashamed of you."

"My ego is fairly healthy," he said. "I don't know that I was ever concerned that you were ashamed of me."

There was something, though. A slight hollow note in his voice. Something that let me know he felt something. Even if he wasn't going to fully articulate it.

I put my hand over his. His eyes dropped to that space on the table. And I felt his entire body relax. Not something I had ever felt it do.

Even after he had an orgasm he was breathing hard, all of his muscles strung tight. He didn't even fully relax and sleep, but in that moment, I felt give. Beneath my fingertips. I saw it in the slope of his shoulders.

I was shocked by it. Maybe that was what he needed. For someone to touch him. For someone to care for him. He did a lot of caring for me, I realized. Yes, it was often in physical ways. But it was all very thoughtful. He never allowed me to be cold or hungry. He made sure to see to my comfort at all times. And that was something that seemed to go well beyond sex. Deeper into something else.

"I couldn't figure out how to have everything," I said. "I realized something when I was walking down the aisle toward you. I had lost. All of my intent was burned to the ground. I had nothing. I was going to be exposed to the world. And then I realized that I was free because of that. That I didn't have to hide anymore. Try anymore." I want that for you.

I left it wordless. Because I knew he wasn't quite ready to be confronted with that in a way he couldn't sidestep or deny. I didn't know how I knew it. Perhaps it was knowing *him*.

He hadn't hidden me for fear of his father being disappointed. He hadn't hidden me because of what it might say about his gender. Or the position he occupied in his company and his ability to do his job.

He had initially hidden our relationship because he was afraid his father would beat him.

And I had to wonder how much of what he did was purely the response of a boy who had been hit when he should have been cared for.

It was almost impossible to say.

"I'm glad of it," I said. "Because I was going to exhaust myself. There was just nowhere else for me to go."

"Except I would've married someone else."

I could pivot here. I could put my own shields back up. But then we would just be caught in the same circle we'd been trapped in already. I had to be the one to keep moving. To keep breaking through barrier after barrier. It felt like a risk. To expose myself like this. But I could feel myself getting stronger the more vulnerable I became.

Like I was becoming more myself as I tried to connect with him.

"Nothing about that would've been a relief," I said. I chewed on the inside of my cheek. "I went to my mother, because if she knows one thing, it's how to deal with heartbreak. That was what I felt, you know. I wasn't just angry at you. I was… I was devastated."

"I didn't want to hurt you," he said. He looked down at his plate. "Whatever you think about me, I want you to know that."

He looked up again, and I saw that same sort of lost darkness there. "I believe you," I said.

And I didn't have anything else to say on the subject. Except that I believed him. For some reason, I thought that might be important. I knew that it was to me.

We talked about business until dessert. And then we talked about chocolate cake, because we both liked it. And considered it the pinnacle of dessert.

"That is one thing I have always resented," he said.

"What is that?"

"The snobbery my fellow Europeans have for the sweetness and decadence of American food. I for one am a fan."

"But you like dark chocolate," I said. "Which is not historically the sweetest."

"I like it at every point on the spectrum," he said.

He smiled. And I felt something like joy resonate inside of me.

Afterward we left the restaurant and he put his coat over my shoulders. We held hands and walked down the streets, bathed in the streetlights. Even this was something we'd never done before. This simple act of walking and holding hands.

This ordinary togetherness that most couples tried

out before they ever kissed. Certainly before they had ten years of torrid sex.

But not us. There had never been lightness for us. There had never been simplicity.

We had been trying to gorge ourselves. Trying our best to have every bite at a feast we were certain we had a limited time to experience.

And now forever stretched before us. Which meant we had the luxury of time.

I laughed.

"What?"

"You're a billionaire," I said.

"So are you," he pointed out.

"Yes," I said. "And it would be silly to say that our lives weren't absolutely replete with luxury. But one thing we've never had the luxury of is time. So here we are."

"Yes," he said, his voice rough.

"We can walk down the street for the next four hours if we want to."

"Well," he said. "It's possible there might be traffic that makes that difficult."

"You know what I mean. We don't have to worry about anyone finding out. No more going through back doors or staff entrances. No more fake names. No more hiding. We were so busy figuring out what all of this meant for the company, and then thinking about… Well, about the baby, that I didn't really think about what it meant for us. I want to know you." I turned to him, standing on the street, holding his hands as I had done at the altar on our wedding day. "Everything about you."

His expression looked pained. "You say that as someone who does not know me. And the problem is once you do, you'll never be able to go back to the bliss of your ignorance."

"Doesn't it ever get tiring," I said. "Playing the part of King of the damned."

"Does it ever get tiring, playing the part of persistent, bulletproof CEO?"

"Yes," I said. "That's why it was a relief for you to pick my dinner. That's why it has always been a relief, to find myself in your arms, to have you be in charge of making me feel good. Because I am tired. Because I needed a place to break down. To cry out. Because I needed to be able to be naked. To be able to be honest. And with you, I found that. Yes, it gets tiring. That's why I'm asking you if it's ever the same for you."

"If it was ever an act, I have forgotten. Simply become who I am."

"But you love chocolate," I said. "And you kiss me like a dream."

"Some girls dream of the devil," he said, a regretful note in his voice. He put his fingertips beneath my chin, tilting my face up. "And some would say those dreams are untrustworthy."

"But they're the only dreams I have."

I realized then that I would give up the company for him. I would give up anything he asked me to. He was more important than anything else, and the actions that I'd exhibited over the past ten years actually did suggest that. I had been willing to risk everything to be with him. I hadn't been brave enough to actually set everything on fire, but I had not protected my position entirely.

I had been much more interested in protecting my connection with him.

That had been the most important thing. That had been the thing I really cared about.

It hurt me, knowing the same probably wasn't true of him. And I knew a moment of deep shame. Was it inescapable, this softness inside of me? Was it a fault of my sex? That I had this latent desire to be his housewife somewhere inside of me.

No. That wasn't the revelation I was having. It was only that if I had to lay out my priorities, right now, the top one would be this. Him. Our family. The life that we were building.

I no longer needed to impress my father. I no longer needed the press to write glowing things about me. I no longer needed to live as an act of defiance to my mother's frailty.

I just wanted to live.

I just wanted to love him.

Of all the things that I had succeeded at, being loved had never been one of them.

It was what I wanted now. Really. Truly. More than anything.

But I didn't say that yet either. Because I wasn't quite sure how.

Because I didn't quite know what to do.

Or maybe I just wasn't quite ready to risk it.

I had risked the company, marrying him. He had agreed to a merger that kept me in an equal position, but he might not have. I had risked my reputation by marrying him. I didn't care.

But I was not ready to risk him.

This was terrifying. It was like standing on the edge of a cliff, staring down into a void I couldn't see the end of. Because what if?

What if he never loved me?

I couldn't think that. But I had to take a moment. A breath. I had to proceed slowly.

Especially when I was not quite certain of my own feelings anyway. Well. I was certain of them. But I wasn't sure of what to ask for. I wasn't sure of how exactly to go about telling him.

I just needed some time. Some more time to turn it all over.

We went back to walking.

"Do you have any good memories of your childhood?" I asked.

"Yes," he said. "My mother. She taught me how to ride horses. We used to go out early in the morning. Especially on summer days. We lived in Greece then. It was magnificent. We would ride through the olive groves and out to the sea. I didn't know then that we were wealthy, or that I was going to inherit a major company. All I knew was that my mother loved me. And the world was beautiful. That is the happiest that I have ever been."

I ached. I wanted him to be happy with me.

But at the same time, I was glad there had been some happiness for him. That he had known love in some capacity.

"Where is your mother now?"

He looked away from me. "Greece," he said.

"You never visit her?"

"I do," he said. "Our shared experience made a relationship difficult. My father made a relationship difficult. Also, I suspect her guilt made things hard."

"That isn't fair," I said. "She made the choice that she felt she had to make, and I can't be overly judgmental about it. I don't know how terrifying your father was."

"He was a dangerous man."

"I believe you," I said. "But now, in the fullness of time, at the end of all things, I don't understand why she would allow that choice to drive a wedge between you."

"Things are complicated. Much more so than I would like them to be. But…"

"You could talk to her. Tell her that you don't want those years to stand between you. If your mother is your happiest memory, then…"

"What?" He paused midstride, and turned to look at me. "Are you an expert now in repairing fractured family bonds, Florence?"

I shook my head. "No. Though I did have to figure out how to maintain a relationship with both of my parents when they hated each other. When I wanted desperately to please them both, and no amount of loving my father would ever make my mother happy, while he was endlessly disapproving of my continued relationship with her. I don't know about dangerous family dynamics. I admit that. But I do know about difficult ones. I had to forgive my father for the things he said to me because he was angry at my mother. I had to forgive my mother for being… For being something I couldn't understand. The truth is, for a long time I was bitter at my mother for not changing. But my father never changed. It was only I found it easier to fit into the mold that he set out for me. If I had wanted to trip around Europe bagging rich men, my mother would have been a fantastic role model." I laughed. "She's strong, is the thing. I never saw it as strength when I was younger. I didn't see how much work she did carving out a place for herself to live."

He surprised me by laughing. "Many people might have taken that route, Florence. It does seem a bit easier than this endless road of perfectionism you've been walking."

"But surely you understand that sometimes perfectionism is its own reward."

"And its own hangman's noose."

"Absolutely," I said. "But nothing is simple, is it?"

"No indeed," he said.

"You should call your mother. Tell her she's going to be a grandmother."

"She's already a grandmother," he said.

For a moment, I struggled to understand that. "What?"

He chuckled. "Not me. One of her stepsons. Also, she had other children. They are all fifteen years younger than me at least. She had another family. I'm glad for her. She found happiness. Less complicated happiness. I am a complicated joy for her. She loves me. I know that. But sometimes love does not look like being able to be there with someone every day." His dark eyes burned then. "Sometimes love looks like giving someone space. Sometimes love hurts as much as it heals. Sometimes love is itself a sharpened blade."

"I feel like I read somewhere—I don't know, some little book—that love was patient and kind."

"I wish it were so simple. I do. But my experience of it has not been simple. My mother and I are both tied to violent memories. We are that for each other. She has a husband who is good to her. She has children with him."

"And you feel like a bruise."

"Exactly that. An old wound that is pressed whenever she sees me."

"It isn't your fault."

"Fault has nothing to do with it." He leaned in and put his hand on my face. It was a surprisingly gentle gesture contrasted with the ferocity of his voice. "It does not matter who is responsible for pain, not when it lingers, not when the effects, the damage, carry on. You can be twisted through no fault of your own, and yet it does not change the result. Blood can poison you. And you are poisoned whether you consented to it or not. And love is not enough to change that."

Somehow, just then, I did not feel like we were talking about his mother. But I couldn't get a firm enough hold on what he might be talking about. It stirred inside of me, a strange beacon of hope that also felt hopeless. Because he was telling me he couldn't love. Regardless of what changed in his life.

He was telling me what he couldn't give me.

But at the same time, I felt like he was telling me he wished it could be different.

And one thing I couldn't reconcile was the idea of hopelessness in this man. This man who was so determined, so successful. This man who rivaled me for success. How could he want something and not obtain it? How could he desire something to be different and not make the change.

It wasn't him. It never had been, not for as long as I'd known him.

So even while a part of my soul flailed in hopelessness, another part felt like it had just had the sun shone upon it for the first time in ages.

He had bought a house with a view of Geneva.

I wanted that to mean something.

"What is your best memory?" he asked, as if the change in subject would shift the mood completely. Like he could control it with new words and a flick of his wrist. With a step onward.

I wanted to share with him, and that was why I let him change the subject.

"I'm lucky. There was a lot of happiness in my childhood. I remember going to work with my father and sitting on his desk. I loved the frenetic pace of the Edison offices. I loved the thrill of discovery. Of innovation. When we would get to go out on the cruise ships, take their maiden voyages, I was always so excited. I loved staying in a new hotel. Flying on the newest airplane. It was an exhilarating way to experience the world. Magical, in a way. My passion for this industry doesn't just come from inheriting a company. It doesn't simply come from the amount of money there is to be made. I really do believe in the beauty of it. I'm captivated by this world. By the universe."

"Do you think that you'll make a flight to space?"

"Yes," I said without hesitation. "Because I want to see it. Everything that I do is about the drive to discover. I really do believe that as humans we will never fully understand each other, understand how to make our world better if we don't see it. If we don't see one another."

"An interesting perspective to gain from the creation of luxury travel methods."

"It isn't all exclusive. We have the most affordable cruise options for the amenities of any other line. We have more flight options and more hotel package options at budget levels than any other large travel conglomerate. We also invest a large amount of money in different charities. Primarily education. Because I really do believe that learning and exploring are the keys to a person discovering all that they can be."

"All because you sat on your father's desk when you were a child?"

I blinked rapidly. "And because my mother took me to different places around Europe. Because I have citizenship both in the US and the UK. Because I was someone who lived in different worlds."

"And you feel like you know yourself?"

"No," I said. "I feel like I know aspects of myself. I definitely learned what my professional dreams were. I formed a lot of my core values from those experiences. I ignored what I wanted personally. I will admit that. I didn't think that I could have it."

I looked at him for a long time. I didn't feel that my expression was terribly ambiguous.

"Why is that?"

"I felt like what I wanted was wrong. I didn't feel like I could trust what I wanted. Because… The most damaging thing that my father told me was the thing he said about my mother. He made me feel like the things in me that might be feminine—that might relate to desire or romance or sex—were flawed. Like I couldn't trust them. Obviously, finding myself attracted to you confirmed that."

"Obviously," he said, but there was a faint smile on his lips.

"I couldn't see a way around it. I couldn't figure out how to take all the passion that I felt for Edison, for wanting to be the CEO, for wanting to please my father, and also…"

"Live?"

I breathed out hard. "Yes. I guess I was more committed to figuring out how to create experiences for other people than I was committed to finding happiness in my own life. I convinced myself that professional ambition and personal goals were the same thing. But the end result of that was that I pretty much only had one thing to claim as a personal life."

"Surely you don't mean sex with me?"

"I do. You have been my closest friend for a long time."

That stopped him again. He turned to me. "That is possibly the most desperately sad thing you've ever said."

Except it wasn't sardonic. He sounded as if he had been hit in the head.

"Why? If you think about it, it makes sense. Who else could have ever understood even part of what my life was like growing up." My stomach crumpled. "Though, I didn't know what you were going through. And I am sorry for that."

"I didn't want you to know. Because you were my escape."

It was my turn to stop and look at him. "I thought I was your loss of control."

"Don't you understand," he said, his voice rough. "That was an escape. It was the only place that I could…"

Be human. Be a man.

It was my turn to touch his face. I did it slowly, deliberately. My breath caught. I was on the edge of that cliff.

Could I jump?

His gaze pulled me into him. And I had no choice. "You have me all the time," I said. "I promise you that."

He looked like he wanted to say something, but couldn't find the words. I had never seen Hades speechless. I was used to sparring with him. I wasn't used to sincerity. I wasn't used to connection.

Nothing about this was familiar. This was one of those intimacy gaps. And we were finding a way to fill it.

As best we could. I had to believe that he wanted it too, on some level. Or he would have simply strode off into the night without answering any of my questions. Without speaking to me at all.

But he didn't. He stood there instead. He looked at me, like he wanted to say something, but couldn't quite find the words.

"I arranged for us to stay in town tonight."

I was surprised by that.

"Really?"

"Yes."

I felt… I wasn't sure. Because this was us, back in a hotel. Not in the place where I was trying to make a home for us. It made sense. Rather than taking a helicopter back up to the top of the mountain, he was giving us a place closer to go. He knew that I didn't especially like the helicopter.

And yet, something about it felt like a step backward. Whether that made sense or not.

I didn't say that, of course. Instead I took his hand and let him lead me on. We hadn't been walking toward nothing. I thought we were. Just walking to walk. But no, he had been taking us to a hotel.

"You're annoyed with me," he said.

"Annoyed?"

"Yes. I can tell."

"There's a lot that I could say about how this transcends your typical ability to read other people's emotions."

"See?" He paused walking. "Annoyed. You were being very nice to me."

"I thought… I don't know. I thought we were taking a walk. It ended up being something more calculated."

He frowned. "Is that what you think? That this was calculated? Nothing that I have done with you for the past ten years has ever been calculated. I wish to God that it were. That would be easier. If I could claim to you that I had control over this the entire time, then… If I had control of it the entire time—"

"I know. You would never touch me."

"As you have said many times."

Gripping my hand, he brought me down the sidewalk with him until we came to the front of the well-lit, lovely historic building with Swiss flags waving over the front.

"Lovely," I said.

He always had great taste in hotels.

"You're still annoyed with me," he said.

"I'm not."

"Do you not want me now?"

There was a strange light in his eyes. I frowned. "What makes you ask me that?"

"It would not be completely shocking. Perhaps it was the danger, the element of the forbidden that enticed you."

Was Hades honestly feeling insecure? Thinking that I didn't want him?

I stopped him, right there in front of the hotel doors. "I want you now and forever. More than I have ever wanted anyone or anything. Hades, I have never even kissed another man. Because I can't begin to disentangle desire from you. I could never want you less."

"But you wish that you could."

"In the past, yes. I've wished that. Haven't you wished the same?"

"No. Never. As I said, if I could have resisted you, I would have. But I have never wished it was different."

Then he turned and walked through the revolving doors of the hotel, and I had to scurry after him.

"I have the key already."

Of course he did. We moved far too quickly through the beautiful lobby, and it took me a moment to realize that I'd been here before.

This was our hotel. The one we had been together in that second time.

"You..."

This wasn't an anonymous thing. It wasn't to disentangle us from our history. From the reality of our feelings.

He was... It was borderline sentimental. I felt foolish. And I felt small. For having been petty only a moment ago.

As soon as the elevator doors closed behind us I leaned in, and I kissed him. As unhurried as the walk here had been. An expression of the shift that had taken place. Of who we were now.

Of who we had been then.

I could remember how impatient we were. I felt it now.

But it didn't cut so deep.

Before I knew it, we were at the top floor. I was dizzy.

I looked up at him. At that familiar face. My lover. My husband. The only man that I had ever wanted. The only one I had ever loved.

I traced his lips with my fingertips. Because I felt like I could. Because I felt like we could have some softness, instead of that endless, driving storm.

It was still there. That storm. But it wasn't all there was.

He led me to the room and unlocked the door. Took my hands and brought me into the center of the living room. He cradled my face in his hands and he kissed me.

Kissed me like he had nothing else to do. Ever.

Kissed me like it was the destination.

I had thought we didn't kiss to simply kiss only recently. And yet that's what this was. The luxury of a kiss.

I had never thought of them as being particularly luxurious. They were an aperitif, impatiently swallowed while waiting for the main event.

Not now.

I focused on the feel of him. Running my fingers through his dark hair. Touching his face. His cheekbones, down to the stubble that covered his jaw. Down his neck, to that muscled wall of his chest, his thundering heart.

It was amazing how this man could be familiar and a stranger all at once.

I supposed, in the way that he was mine, and not mine.

I couldn't say why that thought hit me with quite so much force.

Hades had always been a man apart. Not just for me. From everyone. But I didn't want that. Not anymore.

I unbuttoned his shirt slowly, moving my hands over his chest. Reveling in the feel of that coarse hair over firm muscle.

"We have all the time in the world," I whispered.

The sound he made was more like a growl than a groan, his eyes electric on mine.

He reached around behind me, trying to get at the zipper on my dress, and I moved away. "Patience," I said.

"I'm not patient," he said.

"Because you've never had to be." I wanted him naked. I wanted to see him. I wanted to have him. All of him. With the luxury of time. With all the love in my heart.

I pushed his shirt from his shoulders. I admired every tanned, toned inch of him.

I moved my hands to his belt.

His body was so familiar to me. So beloved.

And yet the thrill could never be gone.

The thrill in knowing that he was mine was endless.

The thrill in knowing that since I had touched him

no other woman had put her hands on him was more than I could have ever imagined. Mine.

"Mine." It was my turn to growl. My turn to grab hold of him. I gripped him tight, squeezing his arousal. I held on to his shoulder with my other hand, dug my nails into his skin there. He looked at me, his eyes hooded. I could feel that I was in danger. That he was only allowing this for a limited time. That he was lying in wait.

Hades.

Perhaps I had finally assimilated the underworld. Perhaps I had finally accepted that as long as he was in it, hell would be my home. Or just maybe…

Hope sparked in my chest.

What if we could be new? What if forever could make us into something different?

And the same all at once.

What if we could be us?

Whole and together and in love.

I loved him. I kissed his neck, openmouthed. He grunted and wrapped his arm around my waist, his large hand going to cup my rear. Then he claimed my mouth, hot and hard. The control was no longer mine. It was all right. I didn't want it.

I surrendered. To whatever it was. To the depths of hell or the heights of heaven. I surrendered.

Because I knew myself. I was more than making my father proud. I was more than distinguishing myself from my mother. I was more than a good CEO. I was Florence. As I had been all along. And I was the woman that had captured his attention all those years ago, never to lose it.

So perhaps I was enough all along.

He stripped my dress from my body, my underwear. Took me down to the floor and lifted me up over him.

"Take me," he said.

I tilted my hips and accepted him into my body. I let my head fall back, but only for a moment, because I couldn't resist looking down into those deep, black eyes. As he filled me. As he made me wild with need.

As the storm began to rage inside of me. Because there would always be a storm.

Always. Because we would always be that. Even as we shifted and changed.

He drove me higher, faster than I had ever gone before. And when my orgasm crashed over me, he pulled my face down and kissed me, reversing our positions. So that he was over me, and I was pinned to the floor.

He kissed me. My neck, my breasts. He thrust into me, over and over again like he was making vows. This time with his body.

I saw something feral in his eyes. Wild. And if he had not been Hades Achelleos, I might have said it was fear. But he was never afraid.

Least of all of me.

When his release came for him, he resisted it. Put his hand between my thighs and stroked me, calling another climax from deep within me before he gave himself to his own.

And the storm raged on and on.

And as I came back to myself, back to my body, the truth loaded up between us. One that I couldn't deny. One that I couldn't hold back.

"Hades. I love you."

# CHAPTER TWELVE

HE SAID NOTHING. Instead, he moved away from me and withdrew. I listened as his footsteps took him away from me. This was different. Different than any other time he had ever walked away from me. And he had done it countless times before. When the evening had to end, and we had to go back to being rivals. When the necessary separation came, taking us back to our real lives.

But this was supposed to be our real life now. He wasn't supposed to leave me.

He might not have left the hotel, but the way that he had pulled away was profound. I pressed my hand against my chest. Felt my beating heart. Didn't feel pieces of it fracture and launch themselves through the front of my breastbone, as it felt like they might. As I feared they must be.

Because it hurt so bad.

So very badly.

I took a breath, and then I stood. Naked. I found that I wasn't ashamed. Or afraid.

I was too strong for that.

We were too strong for that. Ten years, and nothing had broken us. Not really.

We had ample opportunity to find other people. To want other people, and we hadn't. We had promised our bodies to one another all those years ago, without even being conscious of it. We had promised our souls to each other. And I was willing to fight for it now. I would be damned if I let this be the end. I would be damned if I let those footsteps down the hall be the last word on my love for him.

I kept my own footsteps soft as I walked toward him. As I reached the sanctuary that he had ensconced himself in.

"Hades…"

"It is the one thing," he said, his voice dark. "The one thing I did not want between us. And I never imagined… I did not think there was a danger of it."

"Love?"

"I already told you. Sometimes things are simply too broken. People are simply too broken."

"I don't know what you're talking about. How could… How could we ever be too broken? We are just the right kind of broken for each other. Or have you not been paying attention all this time. We are maybe the only people who could ever understand each other. Really."

"You don't know."

"Are you going to tell me that you're afraid you're like your father? Because I've known you for far too long to believe that."

"You didn't know my father was abusive. And yet

you think you have great insight into me?" he asked, his voice fierce.

He was a wall still. No matter how I'd tried to break it open for him. I felt like I was tearing strips off myself. Leaving myself raw.

But I kept going.

I kept doing it.

"You are my lover. That's what you are. You're not a dirty secret. You were not some clandestine affair. You have been my lover for ten years. I have let you hold me. I have let you kiss me. Taste me. Touch me. You are the father of my baby. I know you. I have seen you win battles and lose them. Only to me. I have seen the way that you handle setbacks. I have seen who you are when things don't go your way. You are not an abusive man."

I could feel him resisting my words. Resisting me.

"But I am as easily corrupted by love as he ever was."

"I don't understand what that means." I pushed. And pushed.

"Don't you?" he asked.

"No. Because you don't tell me anything. Because you are… An impenetrable wall, Hades, and you have been from the beginning. You didn't tell me that I was the only woman that you were with."

My own voice fractured. I could feel myself breaking. I wouldn't let this break me.

His face was hard. Stoic. "You didn't tell me that I was the only man."

"But I was the virgin. When we came together. I

was the one that… You never gave me a hint of vulnerability. Not to the degree that I gave it to you."

"I'm sorry—did I never soften enough for you? You didn't act as if that was distasteful to you, given that you flung yourself at my hardness every chance you got."

"Hades… Don't. Don't be hateful now because this is too much for you. Just tell me why."

"It is not too much for me. It is sadly ground that I have gone over already. Over and over again, Florence. Why do you think you weren't the woman that I asked to marry me?"

"The business."

"Little idiot. Do you think I care even one bit about this empire? In light of… You're a fool," he said. "I would let it all burn. Why do you think I made an attempt to set out rules for how we should let this marriage be?"

"Because you're a control freak."

"And why do you think that is?"

"*Stop it*!" I shouted. "Stop making me work for every damn thing. Give something to me. I deserve it. I am the one who has given everything. I came to you. I had to tell you that I was having your baby. I had to stop your wedding. I was the one… I was the one who had to find out you were marrying somebody else. Give me something without making me debase myself, damn you."

"My father found my mother."

I was shocked. Immobilized. The look on his face was raw, tormented. Tortured.

"He found her house in Greece. Her husband, her

children. Because of me. I went to visit her, and he had a tracking device on my phone. He had been lying to me all those years, saying he hadn't known where she was. He was using that to keep me in line. He found her and followed her there. When I saw him in the villa, his eyes were like a wild man. He was beyond himself. He rushed her, holding a knife. I grabbed hold of them, and I disarmed him."

I watched his face as it contorted, as all the defenses fell away, and I saw, not a monster, but a man so filled with grief, self-loathing and fear that I almost couldn't bear it.

"You saved her life," I said.

"Yes. And then I hit him. I didn't need to. Then I hit him again. I also didn't need to do that. He went down, hitting his head on the edge of the stone steps of the villa. It triggered a seizure. He died. It was easy to change the story around just a little bit. Easy to say that he had hit his head and it caused the seizure. There was no bruising. He died too quickly."

"The media said your father died on holiday," I said, aware that it was a foolish thing to say because the media didn't know more than Hades himself.

"We made a story. One that would protect me. Protect the legacy of the company. What was any of it for if we destroyed the thing I was…created for. It was my chance to have control."

My heart felt bruised. Bloody. "Hades…"

"So you see. I am as dangerous as my father ever was."

"You did it for your mother. You did it for love. I

don't care if you killed your father. I don't care if you shot him in cold blood. He threatened you. He held your mother's safety over your head for years and allowed it to become a method to manipulate you by. His death is something that no one is sorry for. He was useless. He was evil."

"It is not danger in the way you're thinking. Look at how love betrayed my mother. My version of it. It made me careless. Selfish. It led my father to her."

I shook my head. "Hades, your love isn't selfish..."

"It is. It has been. It has been all about keeping what I want near me when I want it. And never about giving."

"Hades," I said. "I love you. And I know you. I'm not afraid of you. I have loved you. From the beginning. Don't you understand that? If there was one thing I didn't know about myself it was that. And it was because I was terrified. I was terrified of what loving you would mean. Of what I would be willing to give up. Because the answer is simply everything. I don't care about the company either. Not if I had to choose between it and you. So I never wanted to put myself in that position. I forced myself to deny those feelings. To keep them locked away."

"I wish that was why I kept myself controlled. I will never hurt you. I will never..."

"No. You won't."

"You should be disgusted with me," he said. "You should be horrified. By the manner of man I am. By my capacity for violence."

He just looked broken. Stripped apart by the admission. He had held all of this in for so long.

But I'd seen him look this way before. In that moment I'd first seen him after his father's death and he'd devoured me.

This was the truth of him.

"But I'm not. So, where does that leave us? Because I don't see a violent man when I look at you. I see a man who was abused by his father. A man who was very nearly destroyed, but wasn't. A man who fought for his mother when he needed to. Don't you understand? Your father fought to make you afraid. But he didn't succeed. Instead, you were stronger than he was. You were as brave as he feared you were. He had to keep you in line because he knew that he couldn't crush you."

"He was poison," he said. "If he would have ever known what I felt for you, he would have…"

I saw it then. Real, deep fear. Deep and dark. And I had to wonder what he was really afraid of. He was a man who had started out as a boy. A boy who had been scared that the thing he loved most would be taken from him. Because his father had used that, manipulated that. His mother had left him to protect herself. Left him with a monster. And even if I could be sympathetic to what she had lost, I felt for him.

He was lost in a maze of feelings. A maze of fear. Where he didn't even know who the enemy was anymore. He had decided it must be him.

But I knew that wasn't true.

"Hades," I said softly. "Tell me. Tell me everything."

"It isn't that simple."

"I know it isn't. Because we never could be. We have always been more. Bigger. We have always been…"

"No. We haven't. We were lust, pure and simple. And it is all we can ever be."

I felt like he had stabbed me. What he didn't understand was that for me, his *words* were violence. What he didn't understand was that for me, this was death. I had tried so hard not to love him. And now… He was going to stop us. From having everything. From having all that we could be.

And if this was true, if I had cut myself open, and he had arrived back at the very place we'd started, then there was no winning.

I had no more left to give.

I had jumped off the cliff.

Bared my entire soul.

"What are you so afraid of?" I asked, exhaustion, anger, overtaking me.

"We cannot live together," he said. "We will raise the child, but we will not live together. We will not be as man and wife."

"You don't get to decide that," I said.

"Yes, I do."

"Or what? You'll ruin me? That is where you're like your father, Hades." It was a cruel thing to say, but I didn't care. Because he had to realize. "It's this… This ridiculous need to control everything, that's where it comes into play. You would never hurt me, not physically, but this is a threat. Because you don't know how else to make me do what you want. Because you don't know how else to control me."

He looked stricken.

"You have to… Let go. I am my own person, and I will feel for you what I feel. You can't force me to feel any different. You cannot make me into what you think I should be."

"Florence…"

This was the end. It had to be.

Because if there was one thing I'd learned from my mother, it was that you couldn't let a man take it all.

You had to save some spark for yourself.

For your child.

"I'm leaving you. If you don't want to be married to me, then you won't be married. Technically you will fulfill the terms of your father's will. He won't have won. But I don't have to stay married to somebody who doesn't love me. Because I have done enough contorting to last me a lifetime. I will not tone myself down for you. I won't hide myself, not now that I have just found who I really am. I love you. Desperately. But if I can't have you in the way that I need you, then this really is the end."

Forever. We were supposed to have forever. I hated him as much as I loved him then. Because he had made me hope. And now he was taking it from me. Because of fear. Because he couldn't see past the things he had done, because he…

No. I didn't believe him. Not for a moment. I didn't believe that he truly regretted the death of his father enough that it was what kept him from love now.

"You're just scared. All these years you've been able to keep me with you without having to risk yourself. And that was the thing you really didn't want. You know you're not a monster. You play the part of one well. It suits you. It makes you feel comfortable. You want people afraid of you. You *wish* that you were like your father, Hades, because that would allow you to hold everybody at a distance. You want the evidence of your violence to scare me so you can care for no one but yourself. But it isn't you. Your father acted out of hate. You did it out of love. And you've allowed yourself to change the definition of love so that you can deny it. I won't let you. I won't give you any place to hide."

"Florence."

I stared him down, my fury a living thing between us.

He released his hold on me. I walked out of the bedroom and collected my clothes. I could get my own damned private jet and fly out of here. And so I did, with my heart absolutely breaking. So I did, hating myself, even as I made the call.

I didn't want to leave him. But I knew that I had to.

I cried the whole way back to New York. And I questioned myself. I had taken what I could get of him for so many years, I questioned my own sanity, drawing a line under this the way that I had. Now that we were having a baby. Maybe I should've been more flexible. Maybe I should have given more.

But I wanted to be loved. Most of all, I wanted

him to open himself up to me. To be able to love me. I couldn't be with him as long as he was a wall. In quite that way.

I needed him to be honest with me.

I needed to know him.

For ten years, he had been a locked box. And I needed the key. I needed it.

I called Sarah as soon as I was back at my apartment.

She came right away.

"What happened?"

"I love him. And he won't love me back."

"He's a jerk," she said.

"He's afraid," I said.

"I'm sorry," she said. "I really am. I know that you care about him. I know..."

"I have loved him from the first moment I saw him," I said. "I think deep down I always hoped he felt the same."

"It's not your fault that he didn't."

But it felt like it. It was worse than the NASA contract. Worse than anything. Because I'd had everything in the palm of my hand. And now it was all gone.

My hope, that beautiful future I had wanted so desperately.

I put my hand on my stomach. I was having a baby.

So much of my impending motherhood had been swallowed up by my feelings for Hades.

By the shift in our relationship.

I wouldn't crumble. My parents had lost themselves in their hatred of each other. They had hurt me, even when they hadn't meant to. I wouldn't do that to my child. I refused. I would be stronger than that. For their sake.

"I might not be able to have everything," I said softly. "But I will have better. Because I'm strong enough."

I'd never managed this before. For myself.

I'd gone back to him every time. An addict who needed my fix.

But not now. Because these weeks of vulnerability had made me new. Here I was, a butterfly fresh from the cocoon, with wet bedraggled wings.

But I had changed.

I needed him to do the same.

I could imagine the headlines now.

*Clare Heir Single Mother After Marital Implosion.*

*Every Other Weekend for Achelleos and Clare: Though now it's Custody! Not Wild Hookups!*

It made me want to vomit. But I knew that I could survive it.

Because I didn't care what anybody said. I only cared that for my part, my child would never have to defend themself this way and that to please me or their father. They would be enough for me. I wouldn't need them to hate Hades just to make me feel better. I wouldn't feel compelled to be derisive of him to try and shake my child's opinion.

I was heartbroken.

But I was determined to give my child a life that was anything but shattered.

I had a core of steel. And I would be using it indefinitely.

# CHAPTER THIRTEEN

I WAS STANDING in my office, looking out at the view below. It was Christmas Eve. I was trying to remember why I loved the city.

And then I imagined walking my baby through Central Park. I imagined holding them up so that they could see a statue. So that they could put their chubby baby hands on the leaves as they changed for fall. I imagined Christmas. Like the one Hades and I didn't get to spend together. Opening presents for them. Making a home.

My chest ached and I couldn't breathe for a moment.

I could see it. What we could have had.

If he would have only…

I steeled myself. I wouldn't let myself go down that path. I couldn't.

I had not lost everything. I hadn't.

There was a future there. And it wasn't the one that I had hoped for. But it was still bright with hope. To have a home and a family that had some semblance to what I had wanted.

Because I was the mother, and I got to shape so

much of what my child would experience. And I had decided that it would be good. Beautiful.

The city was blanketed in snow now, the glow of the holiday salt in my wound. Or it had been, until I thought of the baby.

Because there was always next year. Next year I would have this baby.

I heard a sound, the door to my office opening, and I turned, expecting to see Sarah. But it was Hades.

I stood there, completely in shock. "What are you… Doing here?"

"I have come to cut myself open," he said, his voice hard.

"What do you mean?"

"You were right, Florence. I am afraid. And I have… I have done my best to hide my innermost self from you, from myself, from the world, because I never wanted you to know me. The truth is, I feel shame about what happened to my father, but I also know that if that hadn't happened he would've tormented my mother till the end. Until he was able to kill her or someone that he loved. He was twisted with rage. In some ways, I have made my peace with what happened. But I used it. As another reason."

"What reason?"

"Another reason to stay away from you. I…" He paused for a long moment. And I let him. And when he looked up at me again, I saw it. All of it. The truth of him. In all its brilliance. "I have loved you from the first moment I saw you."

"Oh." It was all I could say. A breath, a sound, of pure emotion.

"I did not think you loved me," he said, his voice rough. "I told myself you didn't. You couldn't. It cut me, every time I touched you, but it made me feel safe too. If you didn't love me I couldn't hurt you. If you didn't love me, we could keep it in hotels and bathrooms and coat closets. If you didn't love me it wouldn't hurt you when I decided to marry another woman."

"But I did," I whispered.

"I know now. It blindsided me. It…it made me feel so much regret. And so much…fear. Fear that has lived in me since the first time we touched. Because the things he could do to me if he knew there was a woman that I cared for. The daughter of his enemy? It would've been so much more than him beating me, Florence. My fear over what he would've done to you…"

This was him. All of him. I felt bowled over by it. I felt…singed. Burned by the endless glory of him. Of his truth. Of all that he felt. And all that he was finally, finally letting me see.

I truly didn't know what to say. And then, I decided not to speak at all. I decided to give him the floor. I decided to listen. Because for all these years, I had known him, but it had never occurred to me that he had loved me from the very beginning.

"When you asked me to meet you in your room, I hoped. I knew that I had no right to you. I knew I should stay away, but I wasn't strong enough. Florence," he said, my name a whisper. "When you gave yourself to me, I knew that I could never touch another woman. Not ever again. I thought of nothing but you. After that weekend, until I saw you again in Geneva, I thought of nothing. And when I held you in my arms again after six months, it was like breathing for the first time."

My heart felt bloody and bruised, thundering rapidly in my chest. An endless gallop, as if it was trying to race toward this truth faster than he could speak it.

"Everything was nothing, until those moments I was with you. When my father died, and I told myself… I told myself that I would never put those hands on you. Those hands that had been so violent. I hated myself for it. I told myself it was when I would stop tormenting you. Me. Both of us. But I couldn't stay away."

"I remember when you kissed me. Before we went on stage."

"I could think of nothing else but you. I wanted to push you away, but you were also what I needed. At the exclusion of all else."

I tried to reshape everything. With the knowledge that he had loved me. And it was like I had discovered a whole new thread in the tapestry of what we were. Gold that ran right on through. When I looked at his intensity and saw more than lust, my heart lifted. When I realized that he and I had been coming together because we loved each other…

"I was afraid," he said. "The whole time. That someone would take you from me. That I would lose you. I thought of every reason that I should stay away. It isn't the violence I exhibited toward my father that scarred me that day. It was seeing my mistake nearly cost my mother her life. It was facing losing the only other person on this earth, other than you, that I love. It was a window into pain I did not want to imagine."

He let out a hard breath. "And finally, I decided to marry another woman. With the clock ticking down on my father's will, I thought I would simply cut ties. Set us both free. But when you came to me, pregnant with my baby, it was the perfect excuse to let myself have you. And I didn't have the restraint to say no. I thought that I could control it. And you're right. That is where the danger lies. I thought that I could manipulate you. Turn our passion into something that it was never able to be. Something softer. Something that didn't burn quite so bright. Something that didn't threaten me. Something that I didn't fear the loss of."

"Your father…he used Christmas. He used your love to make you afraid. Of course…of course you feared it. He used it like a weapon."

"Yes," he said, his voice rough. "But I love you. I love you, and it is killing me. It has been, slowly, for all these years. I love you, and I worry that it will be the death of me."

It all dawned on me, like the slowly rising sun casting light over all the shadows.

"You said to me, that sometimes love was too broken. You meant your love for *me*."

He'd been trying to tell me then. But it was all bottled up. Behind a protective wall. Because his father had taught him that loving something was dangerous.

"Yes," he said. "I did. But I realize that my love for you is perhaps the only thing in my whole body that is not corrupted. It is perhaps the one good thing in me. Or maybe I just need it to be, because I don't want to live a life without you in it. Because I cannot want anything but you. I don't want to live in a world where I don't have that."

"Hades," I said. "I will never leave you." I tried to smile. "If I could have…"

He laughed, rough and hard. "You would have."

"I wished away the feelings, because they terrified me."

"I never wished mine away," he said. "Because they were the only thing that kept me sane. The only thing that kept me going. My life was a wasteland, Florence. And you were the one oasis. You were the one thing that mattered. The one thing that I wanted. The only good feeling inside of me. The idea that we could just be together. That we can have a family… I spent so many years believing that wasn't possible. I spent so many years pushing that aside. When my father died, the violence didn't stop. It echoed. Lingered. I felt like a failure in some ways because I felt like I had given in to the creature he made me. He demanded that I marry because he knew there was a real risk I wouldn't want to carry on the bloodline. Because he knew how much I despised him. I hated the ways in which he won. But now… Florence, watching you be so brave, so vulnerable, I have challenged many of my beliefs. He thought that he had control over me, leaving those terms in the will. He thought perhaps that he won the day that I hit him and ended his life with the same violence that he had lived with. But he didn't. Because I'm different. Because something had already changed inside of me. *You*. The way that I love you. He never had the capacity for that. I told myself that he loved my mother at one time…"

I was close to bursting. I hurt for him. I rejoiced for us. He loved me. My journey had shown him how to walk out of the darkness. Just as I'd hoped.

"He didn't," I said. "That was never love."

He shook his head. "No. I love my mother, though. And she left me. And in the end of all things, that is what terrified me most. Giving love again only to have it taken away."

"I won't leave you," I said. "You were my destiny. From the first moment I ever laid eyes on you. You were meant to be mine. I know it. I believe it, down to my soul. From that first moment. Do you have any idea how much time I spent convincing myself that it couldn't be love? We were lying to ourselves."

"Not me," he said. "I always knew."

"Well, I did. I was simply a coward protecting myself."

"I was the same. However different a shape it took. I love you, Florence Clare. Every chance that I ever took to spar with you, to kiss you, to be with you, was just about you. About having the chance to have your attention. To have your eyes on me."

"I love you so much," I said.

I knew then that this was the truth of it. That we had always been meant to be. That our times together had never been an interruption of a path that we were supposed to be walking. It was the real path. We had simply taken a long time to figure out the truth of it. This was where we were meant to be.

"I will spend every day of the next ten years at least, telling you exactly how much I love you. Twice."

I smiled. "Why twice?"

"Because I'm ten years behind."

I wasn't worried about that. Because I knew that we were on the right path now. Because I knew that we had finally found where we were meant to be.

I had always believed that he was my match.

I simply hadn't realized how true that was.

"I love you," I said. "As much as I ever thought I hated you."

"And I love you. As much as I've always known I have. Without fear. And nothing holding me back."

"I can see the headlines now," I said.

"And what do they say?"

*"Clare Heir Lives Happily Ever After."*

# EPILOGUE

*Hades*

I KNEW THE moment I saw her for the first time that my life was ruined. A good thing, that in the years since, I've learned that I can be wrong.

Because the moment I met Florence Clarc—now Florence Achelleos—was the moment my life was saved.

The first time she kissed me I knew it could only be a weekend. But after that, I couldn't let her go. I thought of her when I should have been thinking of business strategies. I planned meetings around the cities I wanted to have her in.

For all the world it looked like the company was my reason for breathing.

But it was her.

It was always her.

I told myself it was all we could have. Stolen kisses, stolen moments.

Now we have everything.

Ten years of sneaking around. Ten years of hiding. Now we've had ten years of marriage. Four children. One very successful merger. But we leave the running of things to other people now. Our family is what obsesses us.

Our mothers make doting grandmothers, and our children are lucky to spend time in Lake Como and in Greece. But our favorite times are when we're together, in the house we bought by the sea, so Florence can always look out at the horizon and plan her next adventure.

I look out at the horizon now. My wife went down to the harbor earlier to look at one of the new ships, and I've been waiting impatiently for her to arrive home. I am always impatient for her.

"Traffic was a nightmare."

I turn and see her standing in the doorway. Like I conjured an angel, just by thinking of her.

Florence.

"But you came back to me," I say, as she crosses the room and stretches up on her toes. Kissing me like it's the first time and the last time all at once.

Even though we both know it isn't.

We both know it's forever.

"Always," she says. "I never could resist you."

We used to tell each other if we could have resisted, we would have.

Not now. Now we would never stay away. Not by choice, not for any reason.

Florence Clare is my forever.

And I am hers.

* * * * *

*Were you blown away by*
Pregnant Enemy, Christmas Bride?
*Then don't miss out on these other*
*passion-fueled stories*
*from Maisey Yates!*

Crowned for His Christmas Baby
The Secret That Shocked Cinderella
Forbidden to the Desert Prince
A Virgin for the Desert King
The Italian's Pregnant Enemy

*Available now!*